TO SERVE AND PROTECT

A TANNER NOVEL - BOOK 39

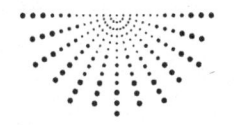

REMINGTON KANE

YEAR ZERO

INTRODUCTION

**TO SERVE AND PROTECT – A TANNER NOVEL
– BOOK 39**

Tanner agrees to be an auxiliary cop during Stark's Fall Festival. When serious trouble arises, it's up to Deputy Cody Parker to deal out law and order.

ACKNOWLEDGMENTS

I write for you.

—Remington Kane

1

THE STORM AFTER THE CALM

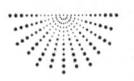

The Stark Fall Festival was underway and looked to be a success. There were games, a few simple rides, contests, an area for kids to pet and feed animals, and even a pair of kissing booths.

The booth with a beautiful young woman occupying it had been active. The other kissing booth had a handsome young man in it, as a nod toward equality. Despite being a good-looking rascal, he had seen only two customers. One had been a teenaged girl who'd been dared to approach him by her friends, the other had been a guy. The young man in the booth had kissed the teen on her cheek. As for the guy, he'd threatened to kick his "faggoty" ass if he didn't get the hell away from him. Both booths were closed after that.

Cody Parker had brought his family to the fair.

Along with Sara, Lucas, and baby Marian, their live-in housekeeper, Franny Facini, came along.

Henry Knight and his grandmother, Laura, were there as well, and also neighbors Caroline Lang, her young son, Jarod, and her father, Raymond "Crash" Wyman. Caroline's little sister, Olivia, was absent. She was in California going to school at UCLA. Henry had also started college, but he was taking classes locally.

Henry and Olivia had decided to break up rather than trying to keep a long-distance romance alive, so Henry was free to date other girls. Olivia had been gone for months and Henry had yet to date anyone. Instead, he kept busy with his college courses, motocross racing, and his training to follow in Cody's footsteps as a Tanner. Henry was weeks away from turning eighteen but looked at least nineteen. He'd put on a little more muscle, had grown again, and was now a hair taller than Cody.

Cody was enjoying his time at the fair but was also working. His friend, Chief of Police Steve Mendez had talked him into becoming an auxiliary police officer. Extra cops were needed to keep an eye on the crowd at the fair.

The auxiliary officers were given radios so that they could stay in contact, and whistles in case the radios failed, and they needed to draw attention. They were also supplied with bright yellow sweatshirts to wear. Across the front and back of each shirt in bold black lettering were the words, Auxiliary Police.

Cody took the radio and the whistle but refused to put on the yellow sweatshirt. Instead, Mendez had given him a deputy's badge to wear. Cody accepted the badge and pinned it to his belt.

The auxiliary cops were teamed up with the regular deputies and given an area of the fair to patrol. Cody had been teamed up with a cop he knew, Clay Milton. Clay had helped to defend the Parker Ranch from an attack by Ordnance Inc.

Cody liked Clay and they had only minor problems to deal with during the day. The most trouble had come from a trio of college kids who had gotten drunk and were being loud and unruly. The boys were mouthing off to Clay, but when Cody walked over, they calmed down and agreed to leave the fair. All Cody had needed to do was to stare at them. The boys had taken one look at his intense gaze and knew he wouldn't put up with any nonsense. They weren't so drunk that all good judgement had fled them. They phoned a friend to come pick them up and departed the fair while leaving their car behind in the parking lot.

Clay had chuckled as he and Cody watched them ride away. "They were scared of you, Cody."

"It's my eyes. They make some people nervous."

"Me included. If I had eyes like yours, I'd be taken more seriously."

"You do all right," Cody told him.

Milton had gotten into a gun battle seven months earlier when he'd pulled over a car for speeding. He had been unaware that the two men in the vehicle had just stolen it from an old woman in a supermarket parking lot. Both men jumped from the car and pulled guns on the deputy as he was approaching the driver to ask for his license, registration, and insurance. Clay stood his ground while being fired upon and killed one of the men and wounded the other. Both men turned out to be escaped convicts from Arkansas. They'd been on the run for eight days and had left a trail of break-ins and robberies in their wake.

Steve Mendez had promoted Clay Milton by giving him the title of Deputy Chief of Police. When the chief formally announced that he was running for mayor against the current mayor, Jimmy Kyle, he told Clay that he would recommend to the town council that he be named interim chief.

Mendez was running for Mayor *and* Chief of Police. He'd wanted to only seek the office of the mayor but because of the town's rules he was required to run for both offices. Mendez had been unaware that he needed to resign his position as chief six months in advance in order to officially declare his intention to run for mayor.

That was a rule change that the current mayor, Jimmy Kyle, had introduced. Jimmy knew it would deter Mendez and others already holding offices from going after his seat. Six months was a long time to be without a paycheck. Mendez had found a loophole in the rule. Instead of resigning, he announced his intention to retire after the election. That meant he could stay chief until the election. A judge allowed that the exception was valid, while questioning the legality of the rule itself.

At the urging of his wife, Ginny, Mendez agreed to run for Chief of Police as well. If he lost the election for mayor, Ginny didn't want her husband to be forced to look for work elsewhere. They had both grown up in Stark and she wanted to make certain they would be able to stay in town.

If he won both races, Mendez would become mayor and Clay Milton could step into the role of chief. Jimmy grumbled and complained about the judge's ruling but there was nothing he could do about it.

Mendez and the mayor were in a tight race, with the mayor in the lead one day and Mendez leading the next.

Clay Milton had been looked upon as a hero after his gun battle with the escaped convicts. The attention and subsequent promotion to Deputy Chief of Police had lifted his self-esteem and he decided to make some changes.

Clay was a handsome guy but tended to eat too much. He changed his eating habits, began exercising regularly, and shed over forty pounds. To say that Clay was a lean, mean fighting machine would be a stretch, but he was as fit as he'd been since high school. Cody figured he'd do all right as the next chief of police.

∼

THE FALL FESTIVAL WAS WINDING DOWN AND SUNSET was an hour away. Cody joined his family and friends at a picnic table for a few minutes before heading over to the parking area. He and Clay were going to help with traffic control as everyone exited the area to head home.

Sara placed little Marian down on the grass. The nine-month-old baby was able to stand on her own, but she had yet to take her first steps. She stood on unsteady legs with her arms raised toward her father. Cody scooped her up, kissed her, and settled her on his lap as he sat beside Sara.

Crash and Caroline were at the table, along with Laura Knight. Henry was over at a nearby field playing a game of touch football with his friends.

Crash had a smile on his face. He knew that Cody was Tanner. It tickled him to see Cody wearing a badge, even if it was only for the day.

There was one activity left to take place. The mayor and his opponent were going to make speeches. With the election weeks away, it was a good opportunity to plead their cases before the voters.

Jimmy Kyle was scheduled to speak first. Since reviving the Fall Festival was his idea, he would be sure to take credit for its success. His predecessor had ended the annual tradition of holding a fair due to budget cuts. Jimmy had argued that the fair could make money if handled correctly. Once all expenses were paid, the festival had been estimated to bring in a profit for the town. Judging by the size of the crowd, the amount projected had probably been exceeded. It was still nowhere near a fortune.

A raised podium had been erected in front of the area where the picnic tables were. Jimmy Kyle approached the steps leading up to it while smiling and waving. Walking alongside Jimmy was councilwoman Gail Avery. The mayor was seldom seen in town without Avery being somewhere near him. To describe Avery as being plain would be a kindness to her. She was bland in her appearance and her manner. No one understood why the mayor and Avery were so close and doubted that there was anything romantic going on between them.

Jimmy Kyle was younger than Avery and a good-looking man with blond hair and blue eyes. The former high school football hero came from a family with money. Before entering politics, he had been in the family business. The Kyles owned and managed commercial real estate. Jimmy's younger brother, Kent Kyle, was the host of a local morning radio show that allowed listeners to call-in. Of late, Kent's show had been one long campaign commercial for his brother, and a venue where Chief Mendez's alleged failings could be listed and discussed.

Those that planned to vote for the mayor agreed with the radio host. Those who were on Mendez's side called in and accused Kent of being biased.

Kent always gave them the same answer. "Of course I'm biased. Jimmy's my damn brother. And I never liked Steve Mendez anyway."

∽

Jimmy Kyle tapped the microphone to make sure it was working, then grinned at his audience.

"I hope everyone had a good time here today."

There were scattered replies of yes, along with nodding heads. Gunfire erupted from somewhere on the festival grounds as Jimmy opened his mouth to make his speech. That was followed by screams and more gunfire.

"Down! Everyone get down!" Cody shouted. At the same moment, he freed the small pistol he carried concealed. Sara laid Lucas and Marian on the grass beneath the table as Caroline did the same with Jarod. Sara also took out the gun she carried in her purse. If anyone threatened her children, they would pay for it with their lives. Nearby, Franny Facini had taken out her own gun. Sara sent her a smile, as she was glad to see that the housekeeper was ready for trouble. As a former member of the military, Franny knew the value in being able to defend yourself and others.

Up on the podium, the mayor was looking around in shock. When the sound of a shotgun blast filled the air, Jimmy ran off the platform and ducked beneath a table beside Councilwoman Avery.

The chief took Jimmy's spot on the podium to get a better view. He pointed toward a barn. It was where a temporary office had been placed. There were also various vendors set up inside like a flea market.

"I see the shooters. It looks like they're fighting each other."

After Sara assured him that she would be all right, Cody sprinted off in the direction that

Mendez had indicated. As he ran, he recalled that Henry was playing football over there.

~

Henry Knight heard the shots as he was about to catch a football in the endzone. He let the ball drop and crouched down to make himself a smaller target.

"Everybody get low or take cover!" Henry shouted. At the same time, he had spotted where the shots had come from. Someone was robbing the fair. The entry fee had been a flat ten bucks a person. The rides charged as well, and more money had come in from the concession stands and craft booths. They all took cash. It wasn't a fortune, but it had attracted thieves.

Henry saw one man wearing a black ski mask and carrying a blue gym bag. He was also holding a gun. The man was hit by a shotgun blast as he was running toward the parking lot. The pellets ripped apart his torso and he hit the ground and lay still.

The man who had shot him wore a red ski mask. He grabbed the bag as another man in a black mask shot at him. Henry wondered if it was a falling out among thieves or something else. It appeared that two groups were fighting each other over the stolen money. The man in the red mask went down from a bullet to the back of his head. The bag was once again in the hands of a man wearing a black mask.

Henry had left the field and moved closer to the action without giving it much thought. His eyes had fallen on the gun the victim of the shotgun blast had dropped. Henry wanted that weapon. He'd left his own gun locked up in his car when he decided to play football.

More gunfire was exchanged before a group of three men went rushing toward the parking lot. One of them was holding the blue gym bag. Henry was thinking how stupid they were to rob a building so far away from a getaway vehicle when a van came rocketing across the field.

The boys Henry had been playing football with scattered before the speeding van. One of the girls who'd been standing on the sidelines watching the game had frozen in place when the shooting started. She had red hair and looked to be about fourteen. When Henry realized she was in the path of the van, he rushed toward her while shouting. "Run!"

Henry kept waiting for the van to swerve away from the girl, but it just kept on coming. He saw that the driver was wearing a black ski mask. A smile filled the hole in the mask where his mouth was. The son of a bitch wanted to hit the girl. His hairy knuckles were tight on the steering wheel as he neared his target.

The girl didn't respond to Henry's shout. Her eyes were locked on the van bearing down on her. Henry smashed into her with a flying leap that carried them both out of the van's way. As they hit the ground, he heard the girl yelp in pain. Whatever injury she had, it was better than getting run over by the van.

~

CODY HAD MADE IT CLOSE ENOUGH TO THE FIELD TO see Henry at the other end when he made his dive in front of the speeding van. His protégé had saved the girl who'd been standing in the vehicle's path at the risk of his own safety. It only solidified the certainty he held that Henry had what it took to be a Tanner.

The van stopped by the barn to pick up passengers. A man in a black mask holding the gym bag was one of them. There were people in view beyond the van. Cody held his fire. He was still quite a distance away. If he missed, a round might strike one of his fellow townspeople.

Injuring or killing civilians wasn't a concern of those wearing the masks. Two men wearing red masks were firing on the van as it sped off. Several of their shots went wild. Having grown closer, Cody dropped to one knee and took careful aim at one of the shooters. Before he could take a shot, his ears detected the sound of a motor nearby. He lowered his gun and turned to see a car come roaring around a concession stand. The driver was wearing a red mask.

Turning back to look at the other men, Cody saw Steve Mendez and Clay Milton arrive on the scene by coming up behind the shooters. Clay was driving one of the golf carts the people running the festival used to get around. The cops jumped from the cart with their weapons out and shouted at the masked men to drop their guns. The shooters did so as the van they'd been shooting at mowed down a section of wooden fencing to jump off a curb and head down a side street.

Cody returned his attention to the approaching car on his side of the field. He stood in the path of the vehicle and took aim at the driver. Apparently, the driver was a lefty. He stuck a hand holding a gun out the window to shoot at Cody. Cody beat him to the punch. He sent three rounds at the arm protruding from the window. All three struck home and the gun was dropped as a gush of blood was seen. Cody had considered shooting through the windshield at his target, but he'd seen bullets skip off windshields before and didn't want to risk a ricochet.

The car weaved then slowed as its wounded driver came closer to Cody. Cody's shots had done damage to the arm and nicked the outer edge of the driver's shoulder. The arm looked to be broken as well as bleeding profusely. Cody was about to place a bullet in the center of the red mask the man was wearing when he recalled where he was. He was in his hometown and acting as a cop. Killing the now unarmed man in cold blood in front of witnesses might not be the best move.

The driver stopped the car and pulled off his mask. He was in his thirties and looked Hispanic. His eyes were wet with tears and revealed the pain he was feeling.

"I need a doctor. I'm bleeding to death."

Cody reached past him, turned off the motor, and took the keys from the ignition.

"Get out of the car and lie flat on the grass."

"Call an ambulance, asshole!"

Cody opened the car door and dragged the man out by his wounded arm. The guy screamed loud enough to be heard throughout the festival grounds. When the scream ended, he lay on his back while panting.

Chief Mendez had run over. He grinned when he saw that Cody had things well in hand. The smile faded as he took in the severity of the man's wounds.

"That's a lot of blood."

Cody pointed toward the gun the driver had

dropped. "He was aiming his weapon at me, so I shot him."

"And did a damn good job of it too," Mendez said. "I'm surprised he's alive though."

"He wouldn't be if there were less witnesses around."

"I hear you."

"How many people were hurt?" Cody asked.

"It looks like we were lucky. We've got two dead over there by the barn, but they're both wearing masks." Mendez sighed. "That van got away with the money."

"This was more than a robbery," Cody said, as he took out his phone to call Sara. "There were two groups shooting at each other."

The man on the ground spoke in a whiny voice. "I need a doctor."

Cody sighed. Dead people were much less trouble than the living.

~

AFTER SAVING THE GIRL'S LIFE BY KNOCKING HER OUT of the path of the van, Henry had continued to shield her with his body until the shooting stopped. After standing, he reached down to help her up.

"Are you all right?"

The girl stared up at him with her mouth

hanging open. She was pretty and had a scattering of freckles across her nose. Seeing her up close, Henry guessed that she was maybe only twelve but was tall for her age.

"You saved me," the girl said. A moment later, she winced in pain and gazed down at her left wrist.

"Are you hurt?" Henry asked.

"Yeah, my wrist."

"What's your name? I'll help you find your parents."

"I'm Chrissy, and you're Henry Knight, aren't you? I've seen you riding your classic car around town. It's a cool ride."

"Chrissy!" shouted a male voice. It belonged to a dark-haired man who was jogging across the field toward them. Henry recognized him. It was the mayor's brother, Kent Kyle. Kent had his older brother's good looks but was shorter.

Kent rushed up and embraced his daughter in a hug. He had brushed against her injured wrist, causing her to cry out.

"What's wrong, honey?"

"I hurt my wrist when Henry tackled me."

Kent squinted at Henry. "He tackled you?"

"He saved me, Daddy. I was nearly run over by a van."

Kent was still staring at Henry. "You're that kid

that lives on the Parker ranch, aren't you?" Kent said the name Parker like it was a curse.

"I'm Henry Knight. My grandmother and I live on the ranch, yeah."

"Look at my daughter's wrist. It's swelling."

"I think she sprained it."

"She didn't do it, *you* did it when you tackled her."

Henry blinked in surprise. "A sore wrist is better than being hit by a van."

"I'm sure she would have gotten out of the way on her own," Kent said. He placed an arm around his daughter's shoulders and guided her away.

Chrissy looked back at Henry with an apologetic expression as she mouthed the words, "Thank you."

Henry saved her life and her father blamed him for hurting her wrist. Henry frowned as he remembered a saying he once heard. *No good deed goes unpunished.*

As Kent and Chrissy moved away, Henry's friends ran over to check on him. One of them held up his phone, revealing that he had filmed Henry's heroics. Seeing it on video made Henry realize how close a call it had been.

Chief Mendez summoned an ambulance for the man Cody had shot. He'd also put out an alert for the van. It was found abandoned not too far from the festival grounds. The men in the black masks had gotten away with the money.

Cody returned to the picnic table. He had rolled up the sleeves of the gray chamois shirt he had on because he'd stained the right sleeve with blood. It had happened when he'd reached in the window to grab the keys from the masked man's car. He didn't want his children to see the blood.

Lucas ran up to him. "Did you get a bad guy, Daddy?"

"I got one of them, buddy. Uncle Steve and Clay got two more."

Sara had looked him over to see if he was all right, then asked if anyone was hurt.

"Just the thieves. It looks like two groups tried to rob the festival at the same time. One of them got away with the money."

Crash caught Cody's eye by waving him over. He was seated beside his beautiful daughter, Caroline. The two of them were staring at Crash's phone.

Cody walked over to them and smiled at Jarod. The autistic child looked away, but Cody thought he saw him smile.

"What's up, Crash?"

Crash leaned closer and spoke in a low voice. "I

sent a drone up while the shooting was going on. When the van left, I had the drone follow it."

"You know where they are?"

"No, the drone I had with me has a limited range, but I did record them changing vehicles. I also filmed them with their masks off, but it's hard to make out details."

"Let me see the video."

Crash started the video from the beginning and handed Cody his phone. It began playing and showed the drone gaining altitude before heading in the direction of the barn. Cody saw himself approaching the car after having shot the driver. As the video continued, he saw the drone follow the black van that had sped away.

The van made a series of turns down dirt roads. The drone followed, which was not easy to do because the van was often out of sight beneath trees that were brilliant with their multicolored leaves of autumn. The van turned off a road and drove down to the edge of a wide stream.

There was a silver SUV parked there waiting. When the driver got out of the SUV to greet the men in the van, it was obvious that she was a young woman, and possibly a teen given her small size. Her long blonde hair was tied back in a ponytail and held together by a clasp of some kind. Whatever it was, it glistened in the late day sun.

Three men got out of the van. They were white and looked fit, but as Crash said, they were too far away to be able to make out their faces, although one man had a full beard. The woman went to the van and looked inside. Afterward, she turned and appeared to be speaking to the man with the beard. Whatever he said upset her, and she began to cry. The bearded man patted her shoulder to comfort her, but soon guided her back to the SUV and climbed into the rear seats with her.

One of the other men climbed behind the wheel and the vehicle was followed by the drone until it weaved its way to a road that led to a highway. The video ended a few seconds later.

"I'm sorry I didn't get a closer look," Crash said, "but I was afraid if I did, they would hear the drone's engine and shoot it down."

Tanner held up the phone. "Did Steve see this?"

"No. I showed it to you first."

"Why?"

Caroline answered. "We thought you might want to take care of these crooks yourself."

"It would be a pleasure, but I'm done playing cop. You need to give Steve a copy of this; he'll track them down. And good work, Crash. It was smart to send up a drone to get a better view."

Crash beamed at the compliment. He was a huge

fan of Cody's. Getting praise from Tanner Seven was the highlight of the nerdy man's week.

Crash agreed to give the chief a copy of the drone footage. Later on, everyone left the festival and went home. The gunshot victims of the shooting war were in the morgue, two more were being held in the Stark jail, while the man Cody wounded was in the hospital. He was under sedation after surgery and handcuffed to his bed. He was being treated in the neighboring town of Culver because Stark didn't have a hospital.

The thieves had gotten away with a few thousand dollars. It seemed a trifling sum to attract not one, but two heist crews. Mendez said as much to Cody when they talked on the phone that evening. He expected to get answers from the wounded man in the hospital come morning. That was the chief's plan. Things did not turn out that way.

2

TELL NO TALES

THE FOLLOWING MORNING, KENT KYLE, AS USUAL, used his radio show to boost his brother and criticize the chief. Mayor Jimmy Kyle was the sole reason for the Fall Festival's success, while Chief Mendez's bumbling allowed thieves to terrorize people and escape with the money the festival raised.

When callers pointed out that the police had captured three men and that an investigation was underway, Kent said that none of that mattered. What was important was that the town was out the money the thieves stole.

"Steve Mendez turned my brother's success into his own failure. He'll do the same with the town if you let him."

With the election mere weeks away, most voters had already made up their minds but there remained a percentage of the voting public that was still undecided. It was a large enough group to swing things either way. If the proceeds from the robbery weren't recovered before the election, it could be seen as a black mark against the chief and convince the undecided to vote for Jimmy Kyle. Recent polls had the mayor and the chief in a statistical dead heat despite the fact that Jimmy Kyle was outspending Steve Mendez in campaign ads by a ratio of seven-to-one.

THE MAN CODY SHOT WAS NAMED DAVID GONZALEZ. He was carrying ID that identified him by a different name, but his fingerprints gave him away. Gonzalez was a thirty-six-year-old career criminal. He was wanted in connection with a three-million-dollar jewelry heist that had taken place in St. Louis two years earlier and was suspected of being involved in other high-ticket robberies.

Steve Mendez learned about Gonzalez when he went into the station the next morning. He had just settled behind his desk with a cup of coffee to read the overnight police reports when Clay Milton appeared in the doorway. Clay had news to give him.

When Mendez read Gonzalez's arrest record, his forehead wrinkled in confusion. "Why the hell would a guy like this be involved in such a small-time robbery?"

"There's more," Clay said as he handed the chief additional paperwork. "We also got back the records on the two that died at the fair. Their records are similar to Gonzalez's."

Mendez read the sheets on the dead men. One man, who had worn a black ski mask, had a record of thievery connected with art thefts. The other one had served time for stealing rare postage stamps that had been valued at over a million dollars. It made no sense for thieves of their caliber to risk themselves by robbing a target like the festival. A gun battle was also not standard for such men.

The two men they'd arrested at the festival refused to give their names and their fingerprints weren't on file. The only words either man had spoken were requests for a lawyer. Until Mendez knew more about them, it seemed a waste of time to talk to them.

Mendez shook his head in frustration. "There's something going on here we're not seeing, Clay." He gulped down some of his coffee, rose from his desk, and grabbed his black Stetson off the hook by the door. "Let's you and me head to the hospital and have a talk with Gonzalez."

THE TOWN OF CULVER WAS LESS RURAL THAN STARK and was home to several Big Box stores. Their population was greater and so was their crime rate, although crime was far from getting out of hand.

The Culver Police Chief was a woman named Brenda Harding. She ran marathons in her spare time and looked as if she'd be reelected easily. Mendez and Clay ran into her inside the hospital's lobby. Chief Harding was coming out of the security office. She greeted Mendez with a grin.

"Hello, Mayor Mendez."

"I'm not mayor yet, Brenda, but thanks for calling me that. I like the way it sounds."

"I guess you're here to see your prisoner?"

"Yeah, and he's turned out to be a surprise."

"How so?" Chief Harding asked. Mendez filled her in on Gonzalez's record. When he was done, Harding looked as puzzled as Mendez felt.

"That is weird, Steve. But it helps explain the high-priced lawyer who's here to see him."

"You mean he's lawyered up already?"

"The guy is from Henderson, Henderson, and Lynch. They're a big firm out of Dallas."

"Yeah, I've heard of them, and they are not cheap."

Harding walked with Mendez and Clay to the elevator. While they waited for the machine to reach the lobby, Harding asked a question.

"Have you had any luck tracking down the SUV that was in that drone video?"

"I sent it off to the state lab to see if they could enhance it enough to recognize faces or read the license plate. They should get back to me later today or tomorrow."

"Maybe that will lead you somewhere."

"I hope so. Now that he's got a lawyer, I doubt we'll get anything out of Gonzalez."

Clay spoke up. "I think he might be willing to make a deal. He's been inside twice. If he gets convicted on a weapon's charge, he'll be facing hard time. It's up to the DA of course, but we might be able to talk Gonzalez into naming names, so he'll serve less time."

"That's a good point," Harding said. "You're going to make a fine chief, Clay."

"I hope so, and I'll have it easier than Steve did once Jimmy Kyle is no longer the mayor."

"That man cut my budget every year," Mendez said. "It's one reason I had to use auxiliary cops at the festival. There was no money for overtime."

The elevator arrived and they took it up to the third floor. There wasn't a cop posted outside Gonzalez's door, but a hospital security guard was at the nurses' station.

Chief Harding spoke to him by name and asked if Gonzalez's lawyer was still around.

"A guy in a suit stepped on the elevator when I got off. That was about five minutes ago."

"Did he have a beard and wear glasses?" Harding asked.

"Yes, Chief."

"That's the liar for hire," Harding said. She led the way down the corridor and slowed when they reached room 314. The door to the room was open. Inside, Gonzalez was propped up in bed by pillows. His eyes were open but staring straight ahead.

"Mr. Gonzales. I'm Chief Mendez, remember me?"

There was no response. Gonzales would never respond to anything ever again. All three cops realized that at the same time and placed their hands on their weapons. Clay checked out the bathroom and found it empty. The small closet was already sitting open and there was nothing in it.

Harding checked for a pulse, found none, and made a face of disgust. "Well, shit."

David Gonzalez was dead. His secrets had died with him.

3

PASSING THE BATON

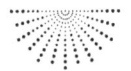

ONE GOOD THING ABOUT HAVING A MURDER INSIDE the hospital is that the medical examiner was already on the premises. His name was Dr. DeLira. He was a small man in his fifties with a prominent widow's peak. The doctor pulled down the blanket that was pulled up to cover the dead man's chest. The left side of Gonzalez's hospital gown was bloody, but not soaked with the red fluid. Dr. DeLira lifted the gown and saw a small wound under Gonzalez's arm.

"I'm guessing he was stabbed by a narrow blade, maybe a stiletto. Given how scant the blood loss is, I'd say that the tip of the blade pierced his heart. I'll know for sure when I get him on my table."

Chief Harding rubbed a hand over her face. "I can't believe I was fooled by that phony lawyer."

Mendez patted her on the arm. "He couldn't have been too obvious a fake, Brenda, or you wouldn't have been fooled."

"I had my dispatcher call the law firm he claimed to be from. They verified that a lawyer by the name of Harrison Ruiz worked for them. I even had her ask them for a description of Ruiz too. The man I met with fit that description."

"Speaking of which, why don't you get with a sketch artist so I can know what Ruiz looks like."

"I'll do it today. I hate that your prisoner was killed in our hospital."

"Not just killed, but he was tortured as well," Dr. DeLira said, as he spoke over his shoulder. He had continued his examination of Gonzalez. "There are small wounds at the base of the decedent's spine. I think he was threatened to be rendered a cripple if he didn't talk. I've encountered this type of thing before when I worked in a clinic in Matamoros, Mexico. It was common with victims of drug violence."

"I saw that too when I was with the DEA," Mendez said. "I bet the torture would have been more intense if not for the fact they were in a hospital with people nearby."

"Threatening to take away someone's ability to walk is incentive enough to tell what you know,"

Chief Harding said. Thinking about it made the marathon runner shiver a little.

"I'd love to know what Gonzalez said to his killer," Mendez said, although he had an idea what it might be.

Mendez thanked the doctor and asked him to call if he found anything unusual during the autopsy. With no one to question, Mendez and Clay returned to Stark.

∽

Mendez's day didn't improve any when he got back to the station. The two men he had in custody had met with their lawyer and revealed their names. They were Alden and Joshua Carrawell, brothers who were thirty-year-old, non-identical twins and lived in McAllen, Texas.

Their lawyer was real and one that Mendez had met before. She had a reputation for getting clients out of difficult situations. That reputation was going to stay intact.

"Reduced charges?" Mendez said.

"And they're being released on bail too, once I've spoken to a judge," the lawyer said while smiling. Her name was Jeania Gaynor.

Gaynor was a former Miss Texas runner-up who

looked much younger than her true age, which had to be at least sixty. Her last appearance in a beauty pageant had been nearly forty years earlier.

"Mr. Peterson and I have come to an agreement," the lawyer said.

Mr. Petersen was County DA, Keith Peterson. The man had often been a thorn in Mendez's side. Mendez suspected that Peterson was bribed. He suspected the same thing when charges were dropped on Royce Whitaker. Whitaker and his men had taken over a town council meeting at gunpoint. Royce Whitaker had also ordered men to harm the chief's wife. Mendez dealt with Whitaker in a way that had nothing to do with the law. It had been pure vengeance.

"What's the DA's going rate these days, Miss Gaynor?" Mendez asked.

Gaynor sent him a sour look. "Are you insinuating something, Chief?"

Mendez smiled. "Just gathering information, that's all."

"The DA recognized that my clients have no previous offenses and took that into consideration."

"Your clients were firing stolen weapons in a public setting with the intent to kill."

"They were defending themselves against the men who fled in the van."

"Self-defense? Really?"

"That's right. As for the weapons charges, the guns they used were not theirs. They simply found them."

"And the ski masks they had on, how do you explain that?"

"It was a brisk fall day and they felt chilled." Gaynor said those words with a straight face.

Mendez scowled, but then broke out in laughter a moment later.

"What do you find so funny, Chief?" Gaynor asked.

"I'm laughing because of how happy I am. In a few weeks I'll no longer have to deal with crap like this."

"That's right. You're running for mayor, aren't you?"

"I am."

"I thought the polls had Jimmy Kyle in the lead?"

"They do sometimes. At other times I'm winning. We'll see how it shakes out soon."

"I wish you luck. Maybe your replacement won't have such a suspicious nature."

"I just call them as I see them, Miss Gaynor."

"You can see that my clients are released once the paperwork from the court comes in, yes?"

"It's not like I have a choice, do I?"

Gaynor smiled. "No, you do not."

∽

Mendez stopped by the Parker ranch after work and explained what was happening to Cody. They were settled across from each other with a chessboard between them but weren't playing. Instead, they sipped on whiskey.

Mendez also gave Cody a copy of the sketch that contained the likeness of the phony lawyer Chief Harding had seen. Cody listened to his friend quietly before asking questions.

"Have you located any friends or family of the dead man who wore the black mask?"

"His name was Marco Deering. He grew up an orphan in Kansas and most of his known associates are in several different prisons scattered around the country. We'll keep looking for someone to tie him to, but I don't hold out much hope."

"His partners who got away in the van are connected to him somehow. And judging by the way the woman broke down on that video the drone took, I'm guessing they were close."

"That's true, but they could have met anywhere. We don't even know where Deering was staying. He and his friends could have driven here from anywhere."

"You do know why the man in the hospital was tortured, don't you?"

Mendez nodded. "His torturer wanted to know who the man's partners were. Now that they're being released from jail tomorrow morning, he'll have a clear shot at them."

"If you stick close to them, there's a good chance you'll capture your phony lawyer. It's possible that he's the same bearded man who was seen in the drone video."

"I'd love to place surveillance on them. The problem is that the Carrawell brothers live in McAllen. Even if I had jurisdiction there, I wouldn't have the resources to dedicate to something like that."

"So, you came to see me. I've already handed in my badge, remember?"

"I was hoping you might find this mystery intriguing."

"It is intriguing. Like you said, thieves like these wouldn't be interested in a score that was only worth thousands."

"There's also the bearded man to consider. He killed the man you wounded. I thought that might make you mad."

Cody cocked his head as he stared at his friend. "Why would I care about that?"

"Um, professional pride maybe. The guy is going around killing people. That's your job, isn't it?"

"Only when I'm being paid to do it; otherwise, it's a hobby."

Mendez leaned forward in his seat. "Seriously, Cody. I was hoping you might want to get to the bottom of this. It wouldn't hurt my chances at being elected mayor if I could say I solved this and got the town's money back."

"You're worried that you'll lose?"

"There was a telephone survey of undecided voters taken this afternoon. They were asked if the robbery of the festival had swayed them against voting for me. Eighty-one percent said that it wouldn't matter as long as I found the crooks and got the money back. I can indicate from that that, the same percentage will hold it against me if I don't get the money back."

"And you need the undecided vote to win?"

"I need most of them." Mendez shook his head. "I never thought this race would be so close. I could lose. If it happens, I'm not sure what I'll do instead. And I'll admit it, I really want to be mayor."

Cody leaned back in his chair and thought things over.

Mendez took his silence for reluctance to help. "I'm asking too much. I know you're busy with the ranch and all and I—"

Cody held up a hand as he smiled. "I'll help you. You think I want Jimmy to remain mayor? No, I was just thinking about Henry. This could be a good opportunity to train him on how to track down people. Sometimes you have to find a target before you can fulfill the contract. I'll treat the bearded man as if he's a target I'm looking for. Henry can also help me keep watch over those twins you told me about."

"I saw that video of how Henry saved that girl's life. The boy has guts. By the way, that little girl is Jimmy Kyle's niece."

"Yeah, Henry said that Kent Kyle blamed him for hurting her wrist. I see that he and Jimmy are a lot alike."

"You mean that they're both self-centered idiots?"

"Yeah."

Mendez stood and released a sigh. "You've taken a load off me, Cody. If anyone can get that money back, it's you."

"How much was it?"

Mendez named a number, then added that the thieves had also robbed the people who had booths and tables inside the barn.

"They made them hand over their cell phones and wallets. They also robbed a couple of the booths that had valuables."

"What sort of valuables?"

"Collectible comic books, baseball cards, and a few old coins and stamps."

"Maybe that was worth more than the money? Some of that stuff sells for a lot."

"I thought that too and checked with the vendors. The comics were worth about six grand and the same is true for the baseball cards and stamps. The men killed at the festival and the man you shot wouldn't normally get out of bed for that kind of cash. I suspect the same is true for the men who are locked up. That means there has to be something else going on."

"I'll find out whatever it is."

"Thanks, pardner. I'll owe you one if you get that money back."

"I will, and I'll do it my way. That means there may be less people breathing when I'm done."

"I've got nothing against that if they're the right people. I also hope you figure out what was behind all this."

"I'm curious about that too."

Cody walked the chief to his truck and watched him head for home. He gave Henry a call while on his way back into the house.

"What's up, Cody?"

"Do you have classes tomorrow?"

"Two in the morning, but I should be done by eleven."

"Good. I have something I'd like you to do. It will be part of your training."

"Cool. Is it a... the usual?"

"No. It involves learning a new skill."

"I'm always up for that."

"That's what I want to hear," Cody said, before telling Henry what they were going to do.

4

A NEW PLAYER ENTERS THE GAME

Tanner was there when the Carrawell brothers were released from the Stark Jail. Tanner and not Cody. He considered what he was doing as work since he was training Henry, and when he was working, he was Tanner.

The twin brothers were grinning as they tasted freedom for the first time in two days. They were sure that they had gotten away with something that could have seen them serving hard time for years. The judge hadn't been as lenient as the DA. He accepted the reduced charges but insisted that the brothers be confined to their home until their sentencing hearing. That involved the use of ankle bracelets that would sound an alarm if they went farther than a thousand feet from their home without permission. Tanner was glad to learn of that restriction from Mendez. It would make it easier to keep watch over the men.

After their initial joy at being freed from jail subsided, the brothers looked around warily, as if they were expecting trouble. They had heard that their driver, David Gonzalez, had been killed in his hospital room. Mendez offered to protect them if they talked, but they had ignored him.

The bearded man killed Gonzalez as an act of revenge for his dead partner. He'd also tortured the driver for information. It was a safe bet that he would target the Carrawell brothers too. Tanner hoped so. If not, it would make it much more difficult to track down the bearded man.

He thought of the blonde woman seen in Crash's video. Mendez had received enhanced still shots from the state police that had been taken from the video. It remained difficult to identify the people's faces, but the enhancement had clarified what the shiny object had been in the woman's hair. It was a large silver barrette in the shape of a heart.

The Carrawells went home to McAllen, followed by a corrections officer who would set the perimeters of their ankle bracelets and reiterate the restrictions that were placed on the pair. The officer was dressed in plain clothes and had a no-nonsense face. Alden Carrawell gave the man the finger when his back was turned.

TO SERVE AND PROTECT

McAllen was about an hour's drive away from Stark. The brothers lived together in a four-bedroom house with a picket fence and a flower garden in the front yard. Tanner was certain their neighbors didn't have a clue that they made their living as thieves. It was a nice middle-class area. With school back in session there were no kids in sight other than the occasional baby being pushed around in a stroller.

Tanner sipped on coffee as he waited for the bearded man to show. Before settling in, he had gone onto the property and set up a hidden camera at the rear. The camera only came on if it detected motion. If that happened, it would send a message to Tanner's phone and start recording. So far, it had captured the antics of a pair of squirrels and Joshua Carrawell taking out the trash. Carrawell looked nervous and had a gun tucked in his belt. The brothers knew that they were on someone's list.

Around noon they had a pizza delivered. Tanner took out a sandwich that Franny had packed for him and ate lunch at the same time. Franny thought he was off at a cattle auction and made him a snack for the drive.

~

Henry joined Tanner a short time later. He wore jeans, had brought his own thermos of coffee with him, and had stubble on his cheeks from having not shaved. He also carried a duffle bag with a change of clothing. They were on watch until the bearded man showed.

Tanner remembered the boy Henry had been when he'd met him. It seemed like too short a time ago for Henry to have turned into the young man that was seated beside him.

"What did I miss?"

"Nothing," Tanner said. He passed Henry copies of the enhanced drone photos along with the police artist sketch of the bearded man Chief Harding had met.

Henry compared the sketch to the blurry photo of the bearded man in Crash's video. "They look like they could be the same man, but I don't think they are. The guy in the sketch has a bigger nose."

"Maybe Harding got the nose wrong."

"Maybe. And you think he'll come here?"

"It makes sense if he's looking for revenge. Why settle for killing one of the other crew that murdered your friend when you can get all three of them?"

"What do we do when he shows up?"

"We follow him when he leaves."

Henry raised an eyebrow. "That will be after he kills the guys inside the house."

"It will be. I don't care what happens to them. They're only useful as bait to attract the bearded man. Those two were firing weapons off in our town when our families, friends, and neighbors were nearby. If the bearded man doesn't show to kill them, I'll take care of it myself."

"I don't have a problem with that. And following the bearded man may lead us to the bastard that was driving that van. He almost killed Chrissy Kyle and it was no accident. He was aiming for her."

Tanner gestured at the photos. There were two other men besides the one with the beard. One looked much younger than the other.

"Any idea which one of those two might be the driver?"

Henry studied the photos, then pointed to the shorter of the men.

"This guy. Other than the sick smile he wore, I never saw his face, but he had some hairy knuckles. As bushy as this guy's eyebrows look, I'm guessing that's him."

"I hope to see him soon," Tanner said.

Henry smiled as he pointed at a photo of the woman. "I'd like to see her soon. Even in this blurry photo you can tell that she's hot."

"We're not doing this to find you a date. Remember, we may have to kill her."

"I get that. If she threatens us, I'll put her down. That goes for the rest of them too."

"We need one of them to get the money back and explain why they went after such a small target."

"Any idea why they did?"

"Just that there must be something else behind it. And whatever that is, it's worth more than the money that was stolen."

"And these two heist crews found out about it?"

"Yeah, then they went to war over it when they discovered they had competition."

Henry settled back in his seat. Twenty minutes later he made an observation.

"This is boring."

"It is. But being an assassin is more than pulling a trigger."

"I know, and I'm not complaining. Like you said on the phone last night, this is something I need to experience."

After another uneventful hour passed, Henry asked Tanner what was the longest he'd ever staked out a place or person.

"It was weeks, a lot of weeks, then I had to wait for the perfect shot to come along."

"I hope it paid well."

"It did, and I had Romeo helping me."

"I like Romeo."

"He likes you too. I want you to spend more time with him the next time he visits. He can teach you a lot. He never had the title, but he's a Tanner."

"Because he passed all the training?"

"He did. It's one reason why he's such a deadly assassin."

"Crash told me that you and Romeo saved Caroline when she was just a baby."

"Yeah, we were your age and knew less than you do."

"How long do I have to train before I take the tests you told me about?"

"That depends, but I'd say at least another year."

"Will you test me at the ranch?"

"No. We'll be going to Mexico. I own land down there that used to belong to Spenser. When you take my place as Tanner, that land will become yours. Tanners have taken the test there since it was first started."

Henry took in a breath and blew it out in a soft whistle. "I have some legacy to live up to. I hope to God that I'm good enough."

"You are, Henry. You have what it takes inside. There are thousands of men who can shoot well and are willing and able to kill, but being a Tanner is more than that. You have the heart needed to be one. You proved that again the other day when you risked yourself to save that girl."

"I had to do that."

"I know, it's what makes you special. Most people would have hesitated or been unwilling to risk their own lives. You simply did what needed doing and never let fear stop you. It's a quality that every Tanner has had. Don't worry about the test. By the time I give it to you, I'll have no doubt that you can pass it."

The bearded man didn't show that day, and the Carrawell twins never left the house. Tanner took the watch until four a.m. while Henry slept, then he got some sleep while Henry stayed awake. The second day was much of the same. When they got hungry, Henry took his car to pick up fast-food to bring back.

So that they wouldn't stick out so much, they alternated between watching from one of several spots near the home. Tanner rented a different vehicle every day in order to avoid someone becoming aware of the same strange car in the neighborhood. When he went to trade each vehicle in, Henry took the watch alone in his own car. They didn't use Henry's car any more than they had to. The classic Chevy Camaro was memorable. Tanner rented a van or some other large vehicle. They would need the room for the bearded man once they had him.

Henry had three classes on the third day that would eat up all his time. He offered to skip them but Tanner insisted that he return home and take them. He reminded Henry it was likely that if anything happened it would be at night.

∽

A CAR PULLED INTO THE CARRAWELLS' DRIVEWAY AND a man got out. He was clean-shaven and looked nothing like the man in the sketch. After walking around to his trunk, he removed a cardboard box that had its top portion cut off. Tanner zoomed in with a pair of binoculars and could see that there were groceries sticking up out of the box. The Carrawells were getting a delivery from the local grocer.

The taller of the two brothers opened the door. He took the box from the man while his brother paid him. After that, it was quiet again.

∽

A LATE-MODEL CAR PARKED AT THE END OF THE BLOCK shortly after the dinner hour passed. It was on the opposite side of the street from the house the Carrawell twins lived in. A young woman emerged from it. She wore a skirt that showed-off her shapely legs and moved about gracefully, like a dancer or an athlete. Her long dark hair hung past her shoulders. Her hair was so full that it made it difficult to see her face.

Tanner wondered if she could be the blonde from the drone video with dyed hair until he zoomed in with the camera and saw that she had a darker complexion. She was also taller than the woman in the video.

From the back seat of her car, the woman removed what looked like a sample case. Along with that she carried a glossy folder that was bright yellow. Tanner was parked along the next block inside the rear of a van. He was seated on a folding chair and had his camera set up on a tripod. Since there was a motorcycle and a sports car parked in front of him, he had an unobstructed view into the next block. The telephoto lens' capabilities made it possible for him to keep an eye on the Carrawells' house while staying far enough away to go unnoticed.

The woman went up the steps of the first house on the side of the street she parked on and rang the bell. Tanner couldn't see who came to the door, but the conversation was brief, and the woman tried the next house.

Whatever she was selling, it seemed no one was buying. She'd been turned down five times in a row when a young man stepped out onto his porch to listen to her sales pitch. Whenever the woman pointed out something in the brochure she was holding, the man's eyes locked onto her cleavage. The blouse she wore was cut low. It made her seem less professional, but then again, sex sells.

She might have made a sale if the guy's wife hadn't stepped out onto the porch to see what was happening. She took one look at the woman and began shaking her head no. Seconds later, the woman was headed down the steps with her sample case in hand. She had decided to try her luck across the street.

Again, she was rejected. By the time she knocked on the door of the Carrawell house she'd been up and down the front steps of eleven homes. Joshua Carrawell, the shorter of the twins, answered the door. Tanner only caught a glimpse of him because the woman blocked his view. After a brief exchange, the woman entered the house.

Tanner smiled. The brothers had been locked up in jail then sentenced to house arrest. The appearance of a beautiful woman on their doorstep must have been a welcome sight. Whether they decided to buy anything or not they could still enjoy her company for a while.

Tanner decided it was a good time to call home and spoke to Sara and his children. He was planning to head back to the ranch for the night while Henry kept watch. If anything happened, Henry was to call him. If threatened, he was to defend himself by any means necessary. More than likely his biggest concern would be a struggle to stay awake.

Tanner was beginning to think that the bearded man wasn't coming. The man might have believed, and rightly so, that the cops would expect him to go after the Carrawells. Steve Mendez had. Making a move on the Carrawells now could mean walking into a trap.

Now that the brothers had been identified, the bearded man could come after them at his leisure. If that was true, Tanner would have to find another way to locate him.

After making the call home and having a cup of coffee, Tanner started to wonder why the woman had been inside the house for so long. He supposed that some sales presentations could take time, but the woman had entered the house more than a half hour earlier. It had still been light out when she knocked on the door but now the streetlights were coming on and there was a sliver of moon on the rise.

The Carrawell brothers had no police records until they were caught firing illegal weapons at the festival. That did not mean that they had never committed a crime before. They were suspected of being career criminals. It was possible their crimes included rape and abduction.

Tanner drove the van closer to the house and parked across the street from where the woman had left her car. Before exiting the van, he checked on the camera he had set up outside the rear of the Carrawells' home. It revealed an empty yard and showed that the back door to the house was closed. There was no one hastily digging a hole to toss a body into. That was good.

After leaving the vehicle, he hurried around to the opposite side of the block on foot. He wore a hood and had a baseball cap pulled down low to hide his eyes and immerse his face in shadows.

The home that was set behind the Carrawells was a ranch-style home. It was dark except for a porch light. Tanner walked up the driveway and entered the backyard as if he owned the place. A floodlight came on as he moved past the rear porch. It was the type activated by motion.

Within moments he was over the privacy fence that separated the properties and crouched down beside a hedge to look and listen.

He heard a few crickets nearby and the sound of a car passing on the street behind him. What he didn't hear was the cry of a muffled scream. There were lights on in several windows on the first floor that had their curtains drawn. The one at the rear was likely the home's kitchen. There was also a light on upstairs.

Tanner moved closer and eased his way around the side of the house. He was wearing black jeans and a dark-blue shirt. He blended in well with the deepening gloom that night was spawning.

He couldn't find a gap in a window blind or curtain on that side of the house and had to move around to the opposite side. On his way there, he tried looking through the kitchen windows. There, on the small window built into the back door was a slit he could see through. It gave him a view of the refrigerator and the electric stove. A big pot was on the stove. Steam curled from its opening, as if water were being boiled. Along with the appliances, Tanner could see partway down a hallway. Through an open door in the hall he saw the corner of a white pedestal sink, indicating that the space beyond the door was a bathroom.

There was no one in view, so Tanner moved on to the other side of the home. There, he reached one of the side windows that looked onto a guest bedroom. That was when he saw the blood.

Blood spattered the walls, the floor, and had even stained the ceiling in one spot. The woman was covered in it as well. She was naked, and she was in control.

Alden Carrawell was shackled to the bed by handcuffs and leg irons, while his brother, Joshua, was bound to a chair with duct tape. They were both naked, as they had been ordered to strip. The only thing they wore were their electronic ankle bracelets.

Plastic sheeting had been spread out on the floor. It was mottled by the bloody footprints the woman had made as she moved around the room.

Most of the blood had come from Alden. There were cuts on his face, chest, and abdomen. His manhood had been snipped away with the use of shears. It lay between his knees on the bed and there weren't enough little blue pills in the world to bring it back to life. The same was true for its owner. Alden Carrawell's throat had been slashed. If he'd been tortured for information, Tanner was willing to bet that he had spilled everything he knew, along with his blood.

It must not have been enough, because Joshua was in the middle of getting the same treatment his brother had received. Tanner could hear his hoarse plea for mercy carry through the closed window.

"I don't know where the other group is or even who they are. I'm begging you, please don't kill me. If we knew, don't you think Alden would have told you?" Joshua looked over at his brother's body. He had to squint because of the blood that was dripping into his eyes from a gash on his forehead. "Oh God. Why did you have to kill him? Why?"

The woman raised the knife she was holding and pointed it at Joshua's crotch. He'd already suffered through over a dozen cuts but she'd yet to harm him below the waist.

A great sigh escaped her as she came to the conclusion that she was wasting her time. Joshua was right. If they had been able to answer her questions, they would have done so. The woman stepped around behind the chair Joshua was bound to and used the blade to slice open his throat. Her expression as she committed the act was one of calm professionalism. The violence neither thrilled her nor repulsed her. It was required and so she did it.

Joshua bucked in the chair and gasped as his blood mixed with his brother's blood. They were born on the same day and now they would die on the same day.

When Joshua became still, the woman freed a key that had been taped to the handle of her knife. She used the key to remove the handcuffs and ankle restraints that had been confining Alden Carrawell to the bed.

Despite the blood and the gore, Tanner couldn't help but take notice of how beautiful the woman was. Her flawless skin was the color of honey and her large eyes were a luminous blue. The breasts were firm, the stomach taut, and the long legs both shapely and athletic. The long dark hair had likely been a wig worn to help obscure her features in case she was captured by a neighbor's doorbell camera or a dashcam. Whatever her real hair looked like, it was beneath a red swimming cap and some sort of gel had been applied to her eyebrows to prevent a stray follicle from falling loose and winding up in a police evidence bag. There was no other hair, as she had shaved that delicate region.

A pair of blue paper booties were beneath a corner of the plastic that covered the floor. The woman slid her feet into them while being careful not to let her bloody soles leave a print on the part of the carpet that still showed.

She left the room and headed toward the kitchen. Tanner went to the back porch and gazed through the gap in the window. The woman was carefully placing the knife, key, garden shears, and the shackles into the water that was boiling on the stove. That would cleanse the blood from their metal surfaces and erase the brothers' DNA from any crevices. Tanner admired her professionalism while at the same time knowing that it deepened the mystery.

Whether she was an assassin or a professional

interrogator, the woman was top-notch. People of her caliber did not come cheaply. Someone had paid her to gather information. Given what Joshua Carrawell said, she'd been looking for information that would lead her to the other heist crew. If all they had stolen was a few thousand dollars, no one would be going to this much trouble and expense to find them. There was money involved, yes, but a hell of a lot more than a few grand.

After placing the tools of her trade in the water to be cleansed, the woman left the kitchen and reentered the bedroom. Tanner followed and was back at his spot at the window in time to see her strip off the clear vinyl gloves she was wearing. They were dropped onto the plastic sheeting, then the sheeting was folded inward and wrapped into a tight rectangle. The woman had left a length of duct tape hanging from the rear of the dresser where it was unlikely to be struck by blood. She freed it and used it to keep the plastic sheeting from unraveling. Once more she reached behind the dresser and removed a green garbage bag. The plastic sheeting went into it and the bag was carried out of the room and into the bathroom down the hallway. Tanner heard the faint sound of water running. She had blood to shower off.

He would guess that she had placed her clothes in the bathroom beforehand. The paper booties and the swimming cap she wore would be the last items to go into the garbage bag before it was sealed. The bag would later be discarded far from the crime scene, and possibly set on fire.

Tanner left the window and removed the camera he had placed in the Carrawells' yard. Then he was back over the fence and cutting through the neighbor's property again. There were lights on and a car in the driveway indicating that someone had come home. Tanner didn't see anyone as he left, and no one called to him.

He returned to the van and grabbed a tracker from a case. He would use it to follow the mystery woman and see where she led him. As he was coming back from planting the tracker, he saw someone walking toward the van from the opposite direction. It was Henry.

Tanner gestured for him to get inside the van. Henry did so, and they settled in the back of it on a pair of folding chairs. Tanner had readjusted the camera so that it was pointed at the woman's car. After he told Henry what he had witnessed, the boy seemed impressed.

"She took her time and visited other houses first. That way, if the brothers had been watching her, they would think she was really just out to sell something."

"I believed it. I was concerned that the Carrawell

brothers might have attacked her. They must have been shocked when she revealed her true nature."

"I guess she's an assassin."

"Not necessarily. There are people who make a living as private interrogators. Sometimes they kill, but it's not what they're paid to do. They're paid to get information. I'm beginning to think that you were right about there being two bearded men involved. Gonzales was tortured in the hospital. Although it was nothing like what the Carrawells received, it was still an interrogation. The bearded man from the hospital might be working with the woman."

There was movement outside. It was the woman leaving the house. She looked no different than when she'd entered it. The long hair of the wig hid her face, while her short skirt and the daring neckline drew attention. Even her shoes had been chosen to lure the eyes away from her face, as they were bright red. Tanner wondered about her eyes then and felt sure that their blue hue was the result of wearing colored contact lenses. As for her sample case, it held the restraints, knife, shears, and the garbage bag containing the evidence of torture and murder.

"I see why the Carrawell brothers let her into their house even though they knew someone might be targeting them," Henry said. "She looks harmless."

"That's a lesson," Tanner said. "Never assume anything when it matters."

The woman eased her car away from the curb and drove off. No one would come looking for the Carrawells until they missed their sentencing hearing. They'd already been sentenced—to death.

Tanner waited until the woman's car was out of sight before following her. He'd instructed Henry to follow him in his car since they were done watching the Carrawell brothers.

As Tanner drove, he thought about the woman and wondered who had hired her, or whether she was working for an organization. Wherever the other heist crew was they had more to fear than being arrested by the cops. It appeared as if they were targeted for death. Henry followed behind the van as Tanner followed the woman by using the tracking app on a tablet. The woman had been looking for answers. By following her, Tanner hoped to get some of his own.

5

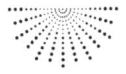

THE GRAB

The woman made a stop twenty minutes later. She had pulled into the parking lot of a busy supermarket and drove around to the rear. When she left, there was a dumpster on fire. Tanner had been following a mile behind her. When he saw the blaze in the dumpster, he knew she had just disposed of the bloody items she'd removed from the house.

After that there were no more stops. For a time, it looked as though the woman might be headed to Stark, but she stayed on the highway and continued on to Brownsville, Texas.

The hotel she stopped at was one that Tanner was familiar with. It was the Victory Hotel. He'd spent an afternoon there shortly after he'd escaped from a Mexican prison. He'd been framed for drug possession by a mobster named Albert Rossetti.

When he left the hotel there were two dead men lying outside his room. They had tried to kill him. That had been quite a few years ago. He hadn't even known Sara yet.

Henry left his car in the parking lot of a nearby fast-food restaurant before joining Tanner in the van. Having Henry along gave Tanner an advantage he wouldn't normally have. Because of his youth, Henry could follow the woman without arousing suspicion. If she caught sight of him, she would likely write him off as a kid. Tanner still warned him to be careful.

"I'll be careful, and I won't be too obvious about it when I follow her."

"Good," Tanner said. "Just find out what room she's in and then come back here. Are you armed?"

"Oh yeah," Henry said. He pulled up his sweatshirt and removed the concealed holster that was clipped to his jeans. The weapon he had was a Glock 43. "I also have an extra magazine in my pocket."

"Good man. Now go."

Henry left the van to fulfill the tasks he'd been given, Tanner remembered when he and Romeo had done similar errands for Spenser when he was training them.

Henry came back with the news that the woman was staying in Room 328. She was not alone.

"I heard a man greet her as she was going inside the room, but I didn't get a look at him from where I was down the hall."

"Did you locate her car?"

"Yeah. It's in a corner of the underground garage, not far from the elevators. She must have switched out the license plates before going up to the room because they're different. There are two cameras in that area and the elevator is around the corner."

"What about our camera?"

Henry smiled. "Check your phone."

Tanner did as suggested and saw that Henry had placed the spy camera that had been used at the Carrawells in the parking garage. It was aimed at the car the woman had been driving

"That was good work noticing that she had changed the license plates, and also paying attention to the hotel's cameras. Are they fixed or are they the type that swivel?"

"They weren't moving but looked like they could be made to do so remotely. Why? Do you want to disable them?"

"I might take that route later if she leaves the hotel and comes back. For now, we'll follow her and see where she leads."

With the possibility that he might have to abduct two people. Tanner prepared for it. He and Henry spread out plastic on the floor of the rear area of the van, cut lengths of rope for bindings, and took out ski masks to put over their guests' heads. When worn backwards, they made for good hoods.

"What do we do with them once we have them?" Henry asked.

"I have an idea of where we might take them. There are several empty warehouses on Military Highway. Once we get them inside one, no one will hear them if they scream."

"This would be some sick shit if we weren't doing it for a good reason," Henry said.

"It's still sick, but necessary. Being an assassin, and in particular, a Tanner, will involve you doing some unpleasant things at times. Just keep in mind that you'll be doing them to some very unpleasant people."

"I get that. If you weren't who you are, I'd be dead right now, and Grandma along with me. You took care of that scumbag that killed my mother before he could kill me too. Brock Kessler was a nasty piece of work who thought he could get away with anything... until he met you. I want to be that person for someone else someday if I can. In the meantime, I'll take contracts and get paid to kill other scumbags. I can do some sick shit if it serves a good purpose. I don't have a problem with that at all."

The spy camera registered movement thirty-six minutes later and activated. The woman appeared on screen looking distinctly different than she had earlier. The wig was gone. Her natural eye color was brown, as was her hair, which only reached to her shoulders. She was wearing a pair of designer jeans along with a modest top and a blue leather jacket.

She was not alone. The man with her was bearded and matched the face in the sketch that Chief Harding had done.

Henry consulted the sketch. "That's him. Big nose and all."

"He tortured Gonzales and came away empty. Then the woman took her turn at The Carrawells. They're looking for the same people that we are. What I want to know is why?"

"That means you'll have to ask them. When do you want to do the grab?"

"We'll follow them and see where they go. If they don't meet with anyone, then we'll take them when they return here."

The man and the woman drove out of their parking space. Seconds later they emerged from the garage and onto the street. A man and a woman, that's what they were, and not a couple. They didn't give off that vibe. They were working together but not involved. That was for the best. Emotional involvement might breed a stubborn refusal to answer any questions if Tanner were forced to torture them for information.

~

THE INTERROGATORS HAD DINNER AT A RESTAURANT on Highway 77. That was how Tanner thought about them, as interrogators, although it was still a possibility that they were both assassins like himself.

Tanner and Henry watched them from the parking lot by using the camera and a pair of binoculars. No one joined the pair, nor did they receive any phone calls. Tanner gave Henry another job to do.

"Grab a cab and head back to the hotel. I want you to wait until I call before you disable the hotel's cameras. If you do it too soon, they may send someone down to investigate at the wrong time."

"Okay. Any advice on the best way to do it?"

"Were they wireless cameras?"

Henry thought about it then shook his head as he smiled. "They're both plugged into electrical outlets that are up high like the cameras. I guess I can just shimmy up the round columns they're on and pull the plugs when I have to."

"That's good. Hotel security will think it was a

prank as long as there's no damage involved. So it doesn't look as if that one area was targeted, yank others loose in different locations too."

Tanner handed Henry money for a cab then watched as the boy headed toward the parking lot of a shopping center that was across the highway. There were taxis there coming and going as they dropped off and picked up passengers from a nightclub.

He went back to observing the man and the woman. They spoke little while eating. Both of them had watchful eyes and paid attention to their surroundings. He would have to be careful in how he went about grabbing them. They wouldn't get inside the van unless they had no choice but to do so.

Tanner found himself getting hungry as he watched his subjects eat. The man had a steak and the woman some sort of pasta dish that might have been stuffed shells. She skipped dessert and had only coffee while the man indulged in a bowl of ice cream. Neither one of them were big drinkers. During their meal, the man had drunk beer while the woman sipped on wine.

Tanner waited to watch them return to their car before heading back to the hotel. It would be best if he beat them back there. If they had plans to go somewhere else, he could always turn around and follow them by using the tracker.

Within minutes it became apparent that they were headed back to the hotel as he thought they might, given the late hour. With the Carrawell brothers having been a dead-end, they might not know what next move to make. Tanner hoped that wasn't true, he needed to get a lead on the people who had robbed the festival. The more time that passed, the less likely it was that he would find them and recover the stolen money in time to help Mendez.

He called Henry when he was nearly back at the hotel and told him the plan they would use to grab up the interrogators. Henry sounded pleased by the strategy and said he was ready to disable the cameras whenever Tanner gave him the word.

"Do it now," Tanner said. "They're right behind me."

~

THE MAN AND THE WOMAN WERE NAMED RAÚL AND Felicia. Those were not their real names but the ones they'd been using for the last several years. Tanner was correct when he called them interrogators. They had both been trained by separate South American governments to "question" enemies of the state. That questioning invariably consisted of torture. Regime changes in their respective countries had led Raúl and Felicia to search for greener pastures. They both wound up working for a Columbian drug cartel where they were paired together. The cartel went to war with a rival and its leader was killed. Raúl and Felicia decided then that it was time to start working for themselves.

They complemented each other and being able to travel together as a couple helped them avoid the scrutiny they might have faced if they were alone. It also helped to ease the sense of loneliness each one suffered. Neither had family and their circumstances made living a normal life impossible.

Tanner had been correct when he sensed that there was nothing sexual going on between the two. The fact was that neither Raúl nor Felicia ever had sex, and they detested being touched. Both had been abused sexually as children. The experiences had left them with no desire for intimate physical contact. It was something else they had in common although they never discussed it.

By traveling with Raúl, Felicia was seen as being off limits to men who might have approached her if she were alone. Raúl had benefitted from her presence when he was picked up by the police. One of the people he had tortured had been discovered too soon and Raúl was still in the vicinity. Felicia had been preparing to torture someone else nearby and saw what was happening from the window of a third-floor apartment. She rendered her victim unconscious and hurried down to street-level. She pretended to be Raúl's distraught wife and asked the policemen what the problem was.

Her cover and supposed reason for being in the area was that they had come to shop at the nearby outlet center. When Felicia ran up to the cops, she was carrying three bags with the well-known names of stores that were located in the outlet center. Both she and Raúl spoke English well although they did have accents.

The policemen immediately rejected Raúl as the man they'd been looking for. They couldn't imagine that a man who could inflict the torture they'd seen would also be traveling around with a beautiful woman. Felicia's intervention had saved Raúl. He had been carrying a shopping bag of his own and the police had been seconds away from checking its contents. Inside that bag, beneath a pair of new sweaters, there had been a rolled-up sheet of bloody plastic and the knives Raúl used in his work.

With the policemen gone, Raúl joined Felicia on her assignment and kept watch while she did her job. They extracted the information they'd been after, killed the poor devil they got it from, and went on their way.

Their current assignment was turning out to be a difficult one. They had been at work for days with no results to show for it. Things were about to get magnitudes worse for them.

∼

Raúl and Felicia looked up when the black van came coasting to a stop near the designated parking spot the hotel granted to guests that stayed in their suites. The two had grown up in environments where danger was the norm and were always on alert to threats. The appearance of the van aroused their suspicion.

One look at the driver and they both relaxed. He was a young man still in his teens wearing a bright smile. He sent them a wave and asked a question.

"Are you guys here for the convention too?"

Felicia was about to answer when she saw something in his eyes. Although he was a boy, there was knowledge and experience in those eyes. She made her living disarming people with various ruses so she could get close enough to them to take them by surprise. Her greatest asset was the fact that she was an attractive woman. A teenager would also share such an advantage. Behind his innocent face could lurk a predator.

Felicia was about to slip her right hand into her

purse for her gun when she heard a sound behind her. An instant later she was groaning in pain from an electric shock administered by the barbs of a Taser. At that same moment, Raúl was getting a taste of the same.

~

WHILE HENRY DISTRACTED THEM, TANNER HAD COME up behind Raúl and Felicia while holding two Tasers. He'd been meaning to hit them both in their backs, but his left-handed aim had been a little low and the weapon's twin barbs embedded themselves into Felicia's shapely buttocks. The result was indistinguishable, and she fell to the floor of the garage while shouting from the pain inflicted.

Henry was out of the van and on Felicia before she could recover. Her wrists were secured, then her ankles, before a gag was shoved into her mouth. At that point she was regaining control of her muscles and it took some effort to slip a hood over her head.

Raúl was similarly handled by Tanner. Although a greater physical threat, he was slower to recover from the shock than Felicia. He was also heavier. After lifting Felicia into the van, Henry helped Tanner load the bucking Raúl inside next to her. Lengths of rope that were tied to the side of the van were placed over their hooded heads and secured around their throats. The ropes tightened during their attempts to get their bound feet beneath them and threatened to cut off their air. That calmed them down.

Tanner spoke to them as he backed the van up to make a turn. "That's right. Just relax and you'll be able to breathe. When we get to where we're going, that's when we'll talk."

Raúl mumbled something that was unintelligible thanks to the gag. It was likely a threat that meant nothing. After that, the drive passed in silence. Tanner headed toward the area where several warehouses were for lease. Their cavernous interiors could swallow up screams and there would be no neighbors or passing pedestrians to cause concern. The interrogators were about to get a taste of their own medicine. It was time to get some answers.

6

TALK OR DIE

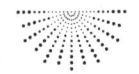

THE AIR INSIDE THE VACANT WAREHOUSE WAS COOLER than the air outside, and there was the lingering scent of machine oil left behind by the commercial property's last tenant. They had been producers of small to medium-sized engines, such as those used in power tools and lawn mowers. They were now across the Rio Grande in Mexico.

Tanner and Henry had carried Raúl and Felicia inside the building one at a time and placed them on the concrete floor in the center of the voluminous space. They remained bound with their gags in place but with the hoods removed. Raúl's eyes revealed the rage he was feeling, but Felicia had remained calm.

Raúl's handgun and stiletto were in the van along with Felicia's gun, which was found inside her purse. She had also carried a small blade. Henry had missed it during his pat down of her. He had neglected to check her crotch area. Tanner had caught that error and used the back of his hand to feel around down there. He'd felt something too firm to be flesh and plunged his hand into the front of her jeans. Felicia's expression had been hidden beneath the hood she'd worn but she had stiffened at the contact and released a whimper.

When Tanner's hand reappeared a moment later, it was holding a piece of tape that had a handcuff key and a razor blade stuck to it. The sharp edge of the blade was sheathed inside a thin piece of plastic. Tanner pocketed the items while speaking close to Felicia's ear. "Nice try."

"I'm sorry I missed that," Henry said. He was embarrassed that his reluctance to touch a woman in such a sensitive area had allowed her to stay armed with a potentially lethal weapon.

Tanner brushed it off with a wave of his hand. "You're here to learn. Now, you've done just that."

~

TANNER SPOKE TO THE INTERROGATORS AS ONE professional to another.

"You two are well aware of the pain I can inflict upon you to make you talk. If you know anything, I'll get it out of you, but you won't like it one bit, and

I'll have gotten bloody and will need to change my clothes. Instead of that, why don't you tell me everything you know. If you do that, I'll let you live, and we can go our separate ways."

After speaking, Tanner nodded at Henry. Henry removed the gag on Felicia as Tanner released the one on Raúl.

Raúl began talking the instant he was able. "You'll kill us no matter what happens here."

"No. I'll only kill you if you refuse to talk to me or if I'm certain that you're lying to me. I know what and who the two of you are. I also know that what you do to those you question isn't personal. This isn't personal for me either. I want information. I don't need to take your lives unless I have to."

Raúl looked over at Felicia, then back at Tanner. "If you harm her, I will kill you."

Tanner raised an eyebrow as those words were spoken. There was passion in the man's voice. It seemed that there was something between them after all. He looked over at the woman and saw confusion in her eyes. Raúl's emotional display had surprised her. Raúl's affection was one-sided.

Tanner sighed. "I won't have to hurt either of you if you start talking. You can begin by telling me your names."

The woman spoke, revealing a light Spanish

accent. "I am Felicia and he is Raúl. What is your name?"

"My name doesn't matter," Tanner said. He didn't need the word getting out that he was in Texas. If that happened often enough, someone might realize he lived in the state, and not in New York City, where he had been most active.

"Who do you work for?" Tanner asked Felicia.

"We do not know the client's name. Everything is handled over the internet. We get a flat fee and if we're successful, we're paid more."

"I saw the end of your... discussion, with the Carrawell brothers. You're looking for the heist crew that robbed the Fall Festival in Stark, Texas. I'm looking for them too. I know my reasons, what are yours?"

"Don't tell him a damn thing, Felicia," Raúl said.

"You should want her to tell me. I wasn't lying when I said that I would let you live if you told me what you know. The opposite is true if you don't tell me."

Raúl cursed at Tanner and issued an order. "Release her now and I'll tell you what you want to know."

Tanner ignored him and spoke to Felicia again. "Why are you looking for the heist crew?"

"They stole something valuable that was to be passed on to someone else. The item is an old and rare piece of United States currency, a thousand-dollar bill from 1880. We were told that it's valued at nearly two million dollars."

Tanner gave her answer some thought before asking, "Does this involve money laundering?"

Felicia nodded. "I wasn't told that but it's what I believe. It's been done with old stamps, artwork, diamonds, and antique coins. The rare bill would work just as well."

Tanner stared at her. He believed she was telling the truth.

"How did the two heist crews learn about the bill?"

"I do not know about the people we seek, but Alden Carrawell told me that he was tipped off by the man the currency was stolen from. He is a dealer in old stamps and coins who had a booth at the festival. Carrawell, his brother, and two others were to pay him twenty percent of the bill's value after they found a buyer. Instead, the other group robbed him. When the Carrawells arrived, they saw that the other thieves had struck first and they fought."

"What's the name of this dealer in old stamps?"

"Alex Tinsley. He has a shop in a town nearby named Culver."

"I guess he would have been your next target, hmm?"

Felicia hesitated just an instant before nodding.

Tanner wondered about her delay in answering but pressed on with his questions.

"Who was Tinsley supposed to pass the bill on to if there had been no robbery?"

"I don't know. It must have been someone involved in the money laundering."

"Are they the same people who hired you?"

"She already told you that we don't know who hired us, maricón," Raúl spat.

Tanner looked at him and saw the hatred in his eyes. "You're taking this personally. I was hoping we could keep this on a professional level."

Felicia looked over at her partner. "We have nothing to gain by angering this man or lying to him. He says he'll let us live and I believe him."

"He's lying. If he let us live, he knows that I would hunt him down and kill him."

Tanner looked at Felicia. "Will you come looking for me too?"

"No. I will leave this area as soon as I can. But I warn you, the people who hired us will send others in our place. They will not give up on finding what belongs to them. They'll also punish anyone involved. That includes you and your young friend here," Felicia said, then looked at Henry. The teen stared back at her until she looked away.

"Raúl," Tanner said.

Raúl glared at him. "What?"

"You should never have threatened me." Tanner drew his gun and fired at Raúl with such speed that the man didn't have time to react before the bullet struck him in the forehead.

Felicia gasped in shock. Her astonishment was not surprise at Raúl dying, but at Tanner's speed with the gun. He'd cleared leather, fired the shot, and had the gun holstered again in less than a second.

Henry gave a little shake of his head. He was fast with a gun, but not that damn fast. Seeing his mentor in action reminded him of just how big the shoes were that he hoped to fill someday. Cody might be the seventh Tanner, but he was one of a kind.

Felicia tore her gaze away from Raúl's dead form. "I've told you everything I know. What happens now?"

Tanner reached into his pocket and took out the razor blade he'd found on Felicia. He dropped it on the floor in front of her.

"You should be able to free yourself with that. Afterward, get far away from here. If I see you again, I'll assume that you're looking for me and I'll kill you. Understand?"

"Yes," Felicia said.

Tanner nodded at Henry and the two of them headed for the exit.

FELICA GLANCED OVER AT RAÚL'S CORPSE AGAIN before maneuvering her hands around to where she could grab the razor blade. By the time she freed herself and made it out of the warehouse the van was gone. Her purse had been left near the door. It contained her wallet, keys, and passport. Her phone was missing and so was her gun. She couldn't remember the last time she didn't have a gun handy and was grateful that she still had the razor blade.

A few hundred yards away were the lights of the cars on the roadway. Felicia began walking toward them. Thirty-one minutes later a vintage pickup truck pulled over and an old man with kind eyes was looking at her with an expression of concern. He was wrinkled and sunburned. Despite his age, his clothes were the attire of a working man. His hands looked like his callouses had callouses.

"Young lady, are you all right?"

Felicia gave him a sad smile. "I just broke up with my boyfriend and he made me get out of his car."

The old man gawked at her. "Out here? At night?"

She nodded and saw the man color with anger.

"Hop in and I'll take you where you want to go."

Felicia climbed into the truck. "Thank you. Is there an airport near here?"

"Oh yeah. It's not far at all. Is that where you want to go?"

"Yes."

"I'll have you there in a jiffy. My name is Terry Rowan. What's your name?"

"Felicia."

"It's nice to meet you, missy. Are you planning on flying back home?"

Felicia nodded yes but it was a lie. Home had been a slum where her mother had sold her to men for sex to get drugs. Felicia had left there at thirteen and never looked back.

Terry dropped her off at the airport and wished her luck. While she was waiting for her flight, Felicia stole a phone from a man in the airport bar whose rapt attention was on the game playing on the TV. The phone's screen was unlocked, and she was able to send a message to the people she and Raúl were working for.

The leads we had all turned out to be dead ends. I'm willing to work for you again in the future but no more on this one. My partner was killed by an unknown man who is looking for the same people. This man is very dangerous. He is about six-feet tall with dark hair and has eyes that make one shiver. I suggest you take him seriously and send someone to deal with him. You might want to send more than one.

She opened the message with a code word that

identified her and ended it with the same word. Before getting on her plane, Felicia dumped the stolen phone in a garbage can. She was flying to San Antonio because that was the first plane available. She'd stay there overnight and head to Miami where she could get a new set of ID. She was done with being Felicia.

She thought of Raúl. He had displayed genuine concern for her welfare, yet she was convinced that he hadn't been infatuated with her. The man had never even hinted at anything like that in the six years they'd worked together. Perhaps he'd been motivated by a sense of machismo. A part of her would miss him.

Then she thought about Tanner. She had been certain he was lying about letting her live but saw no reason to refuse to answer his questions. That would have only made things harder on her. When he tossed her the razor blade so that she could free herself it surprised her. She had never before met anyone who kept their word.

She thought about the message she'd sent and wondered if she should have mentioned that Tanner wasn't alone and that he had a boy helping him. No. Let him have that small edge. Felicia surprised herself by having that thought and realized she wanted Tanner to win.

That would not happen. The people she worked

for were not the type to lose. They would send someone to deal with Tanner. More than one, as she suggested, and they would see to it that he stopped interfering in their business.

Felicia spent most of the flight considering what new name she would go by. She decided that she would choose Natasha. She'd always liked the sound of it.

7

TRAPPED

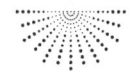

It was after ten by the time Cody made it home and, of course, the kids were both asleep. He was Cody at home. Until he left to run down another lead, Tanner would be put on hold.

Sara was awake in the living room and cleaning a pistol while she watched a movie on TV. She'd been practicing her shooting at their indoor range and had gone through several boxes of brass.

After greeting each other with a kiss, Sara paused the movie and asked Cody if he was hungry.

"I am. I haven't eaten since lunch."

"Franny always has something good in the refrigerator. I'll heat you up something."

The food turned out to be chicken and dumplings. Franny made them the same way Cody's mother used to make the dish when he was a kid.

As he ate, Sara indulged by eating two chocolate chip cookies. Those she had made herself. After eating, they returned to the living room. Sara stretched out across the sofa while resting her head on Cody's lap. While he talked and told her about his recent activities, Cody ran his hands through her hair.

As he was partway through relaying the Carrawell brothers' worst day ever, Sara asked for clarification on one point.

"She tortured them while she was naked?"

"Yeah."

"What does she look like?"

"Young, beautiful, with flawless skin."

"Not that you noticed, hmm? She gave you quite an eyeful, didn't she?"

"She did at that."

"Getting naked in front of men you're torturing sounds like some sort of kinky sexual deviancy. I wonder if she got a thrill out of it."

"You can be sure the men didn't."

Cody finished telling Sara the rest of the story and she made an observation.

"It sounds like you're no closer to finding the robbers than you were before."

"It sounds like that because it's true, but I've another lead to look into."

"Tonight?"

"No. Tonight I'm sleeping here, and, in the morning, I'll have breakfast with you and the kids."

Sara grinned as she sat up, then made it to her feet, as she took Cody by the hand. "Let's go to bed."

"I could use the sleep."

"You won't get as much sleep as you think. You're about to see another naked lady—me."

"Do you plan on torturing me too?"

"If that's what you want."

"Talk about kinky," Cody said, and Sara laughed.

∼

Henry had classes again and Tanner told him to relax afterwards or catch up on his studying. Until he had a firm direction to head in, there was no point in them both running around chasing their tails.

There was one lead that Tanner could look into, the vendor whom the rare bill had been stolen from, Alex Tinsley. Felicia had said that Tinsley was involved with his own robbery and had made a deal with the Carrawells. If her employers had that information Tinsley was either dead or on the run. And while it was unlikely that he would know anything about the other crew that had the stolen item, the lead had to be checked out.

After rising early for a ten-mile run and an

intense calisthenics workout, Cody had breakfast with his family. Later on, he had a brief meeting with Rick Winhoffer, the foreman of his ranch. Rick wanted to let Cody know that they would have more than enough silage stored for feeding the cattle during winter. There were also discussions about ranch employees. One in particular was Elijah Turner. Elijah was a friend of the ranch house's caretaker, Bobby Lincoln, and was also dating Winhoffer's daughter, Heidi.

"You have concerns about Elijah, Rick?"

"Not at all. He's become my right-hand man, and I've gotten to know him and his family on a personal level because of how close he and Heidi have become."

"Okay, so what did you want to talk about?"

"I'd like to promote him to the position of Assistant Ranch Foreman."

"That position doesn't exist."

"It could, with your say so. But it will also require giving Elijah a bump in pay."

Cody grinned. "It sounds good to me. I've seen how hard he works around here. I'd hate to lose him to another ranch."

"So would I," Winhoffer said. "And Heidi would give me hell if that happened."

"I don't think Elijah is going anywhere without

Heidi. If anything, you might have him as a son-in-law someday."

"I could do worse. He's a damn good man. Do you want to give him the news about the promotion or should I?"

"You do it," Cody said. "And bump his pay up by forty percent. Just let him know that he'll have more responsibility now too."

"Oh yeah he will; I'll be training him to take my place someday. It's smart business to always have someone who can fill in for you when you're laid up or off on a vacation. And someday when I retire, it will be nice to know that things are in good hands."

"I agree," Cody said, as he thought about his training of Henry to succeed him as Tanner.

Cody had other matters to attend to that concerned the ranch and his personal affairs. When he was done with them it was time for lunch. He ate while also feeding his baby daughter, Marian, then saddled up a horse and took a ride around the property with Lucas. As he rode, an idea came to him that might result in getting a fresh lead on the thieves who robbed the festival.

After returning to the house, he settled in the office and called Kate Barlow.

"How can I help you, Tanner?"

"Do you know anyone who can enhance and enlarge stills from video?"

"I can do that."

"Do you have the time?"

"For you? Always."

"Thank you, Kate. I'll send you the video. It shows a young girl being knocked out of the path of a speeding van. See if you can get a clearer look at the driver. He's wearing a mask, so it won't be easy. I also need a sharper view of the people in the background that are near a barn. Some of those people will be masked too, but I'm hoping to find something that might lead me to them."

"I'll get on this as soon as you send me the video."

There was a voice in the background on Kate's end. Tanner recognized that it was Kate's husband, Michael. He was speaking to someone and did not sound happy.

"What's Michael so angry about?"

"Oh, he's on the phone with our son. We called to say happy birthday and now it's turned into an argument."

"How does that happen?"

Kate sighed. "Our son, and our daughter have asked us to never speak to them again. We didn't think that meant we couldn't call on their birthdays."

"I doubt Michael's shouting is making things

better."

"No, but my husband and my son are both stubborn, and at least they're talking."

"I'll be waiting to see what you turn up on that video, and don't forget to bill me this time."

"We owe you our lives, Tanner. A favor here and there is nothing."

∽

TANNER STAYED HOME UNTIL THE KIDS WERE LAID down for their naps before he left to continue his search on the robbers.

He arrived at Alex Tinsley's shop in Culver just before three p.m. The sign over the door stated that the shop dealt in *Numismatics & Philately*. In other words, currency and stamps.

It didn't surprise Tanner to find that the shop was closed. If Tinsley had any sense, he was out of the country by now. Wanting to be thorough, Tanner decided to enter the shop and look around. That was when he discovered that someone else had that idea already.

The back door had been left unlocked. After entering, Tanner saw that the face of the alarm system's control panel had been removed. Some of the exposed wires had small alligator clips attached while others had been snipped.

The back door opened onto an office with an L-shaped desk. There was also a mini fridge, coffee maker, and a floor safe that was sitting open and was empty. A small bathroom in a corner was barely big enough to hold the sink and toilet inside it.

As he left the office, Tanner looked left and saw a table and two chairs inside a small room. On the table was a powerful electronic magnifying glass. The device had a pair of bright LED lights attached. It was where Tinsley would let serious customers with money take a private gander at the valuable currency or stamps they were thinking of buying.

The rest of the shop had glass cases containing the regular merchandise while stamp and coin collecting paraphernalia filled several racks and hung from hooks on the walls behind a counter.

Whoever searched the shop had done a thorough job. Books were piled up on the floor and it was a safe bet that every one of them had been searched for the valuable 1880 thousand-dollar bill.

There were other pieces of old currency in the shop. They were sealed in clear, rigid vinyl sleeves or otherwise protected. They had been scrutinized and left stacked on a counter near the cash register. Every drawer had been opened, every rack shuffled through, and the ceiling tile had been moved around and the toilet tank in the bathroom peeked into.

Tanner remembered Felicia's hesitation when

he'd stated that Tinsley would have been their next target. She must have known that Raúl had already attended to that matter. While she was torturing and killing the Carrawells, Raúl had been searching for Tinsley and rummaging through his shop.

Before he got off the phone with Kate Barlow, Tanner had asked Kate to see what she could find on Tinsley. She had sent him a text back minutes later.

Alex Tinsley had recently sold his home and had a buyer lined up for the shop. He was sixty-eight and had been ready to pack it in and ride off into the sunset. Arranging to have the rare bill stolen was a way to enhance his retirement fund. He grossly underestimated the gullibility of the people he'd been laundering funds for. Even if he had nothing to do with the heist, they would have assumed he had and sent someone to question him. Now that Alden Carrawell had claimed that Tinsley was involved, there was nowhere he could hide. That didn't mean he wouldn't try.

Kate had found an address for Tanner to check out. It belonged to Tinsley's only daughter. She was recently divorced and living under the surname of Weiss, in Corpus Christi. That was Tanner's next stop.

Alex Tinsley's daughter, Julie Weiss, lived among a row of two-story homes in Corpus Christi that had green front lawns and attached garages. Dusk had settled on the community by the time Tanner arrived in the city.

He drove past Julie Weiss's house, parked around the block, and returned on foot while pretending to be a jogger out for a run. Tanner looked the part with the dark-blue jogging outfit and black sneakers he was wearing. There were also a pair of earphones to enhance the look but there was no music playing through them.

The homes he moved past were alive inside with activity as the evening meal was being prepared for those, and by those, who had recently returned home from a hard day at work. If there were children in the neighborhood none were in view, but then, the days of kids playing hopscotch and kick the can on the neighborhood sidewalks were in the past. Most of the current crop of youths had probably never even heard of the games, much less played them.

Tanner stopped running in front of Weiss's driveway and looked around while appearing to tie an errant shoelace. There was a light aglow in the front windows of the home indicating that someone might be inside. There was also a car parked at the top of the driveway. It was a late-model green

Mercedes. The license plate matched the one Kate Barlow had given Tanner for Tinsley's car. He had located the dealer in rare items.

Tanner continued on his run and jogged past the house. There were very few cars on the street as most of them were in garages or parked in the owner's driveway. The traffic driving through the neighborhood was sporadic as the street became a dead-end three blocks to the north.

He saw no one sitting in a car as if they were keeping watch and there was no one peering out from a window. After reaching the corner, Tanner turned around and ran back the way he had come. He slowed his pace to allow a man across the street and three houses away to head back up his front steps after checking his mailbox, which was at the curb. As soon as the man's back was to him, Tanner quickened his steps and rushed up Weiss's driveway, past the Mercedes, and into the backyard.

He heard no voices but there was the sound of a television playing. The blinds on the kitchen windows had yet to be lowered and he could see that there were two pans on the stove. The small table in the kitchen had place settings already. It appeared as if dinner was soon to be served.

Tanner was ready to pick the lock on the rear door but found it wasn't necessary. The door was unlocked. As he eased open the door, he could hear the TV and discerned that there was a news station playing. He lowered the shades on the kitchen windows. Maybe Tinsley's daughter didn't like privacy, but he did.

He still had yet to hear any voices but that didn't mean anything since there were probably only two people in the home. If they were in separate rooms, they wouldn't be talking.

The kitchen smelled strongly of coffee. Instead of being pleasant, the odor was harsh. A look at the coffee maker on the counter revealed that the bottom of the carafe was a dark brown. It appeared that someone had left the coffee maker on when there was barely any brew left in it. What little remained was overheated and burned until the machine's automatic shutoff kicked in. That usually took four hours.

Tanner left the kitchen to step into a dimly lit hallway. That was when he detected a second odor, one he had smelled too many times before. It wasn't the sick odor of decay, not yet, but it was the scent of recent death.

Tanner moved deeper into the house with his gun in his hand and found the bodies in the living room. Alex Tinsley had a head of white hair and was dressed in a green robe. His daughter was blonde, her robe was pink, but her blood, and that of her father was red and a great deal of it was no longer in their bodies. The table in the kitchen wasn't set for dinner, it had been set for breakfast.

Tinsley had been tortured and was missing several fingers on his right hand. His daughter had been gagged and appeared to have been violated with an instrument. A bloodstained rolling pin was on the floor between her legs. The daughter had been tortured to make Tinsley talk after the loss of several fingers had seemed inadequate. A knife blade across her throat had finished her.

One look at the scene told Tanner that there had to have been more than one person involved. Tinsley hadn't been restrained. There were no marks on his wrists that would indicate handcuffs or other ligatures. There was bruising above the right wrist where hands had held him while someone else cut away his fingers.

Tanner killed the TV and moved around the rest of the home until he was certain he was alone. When he returned to the kitchen to leave, he shut off the ceiling lights and saw the red light blinking on the small device above the doorframe. He had taken it to be a smoke alarm when he'd first seen it upon entering but now knew it for what it was. It was a motion detector. Someone knew he was in the house.

The sound of a car pulling into the driveway came an instant before the squeal of brakes, the opening and closing of car doors, and the distinctive sounds of shotguns being cocked.

Tanner saw a shadow sprint past a window. Someone had run to the rear of the house to block his exit through the back door. Tanner moved into the living room again and could see that headlights were aimed at the front of the house. He moved to the side of a window to look out and saw two men standing near the foot of the front steps. They were tall, had military buzz cuts, and wore ankle duster, black leather coats with snakeskin boots. Each man carried a shotgun, and not just any shotgun. They were Benelli M4s. They were partially hidden within the folds of the coats. If the men were viewed from the side or from behind, you wouldn't know they were armed.

One of the men reached through the open window of the car to dim the lights but left the engine running. The vehicle was a black 1969 Dodge Charger. Between the coats, the guns, and the car, Tanner had to admit they had style.

The man who had dimmed the car's lights spoke in a clear voice that wasn't loud but could be heard plainly over the sound of the Charger's engine.

"Either you come out or we come in. What will it be?"

Tanner smiled. Maybe now he would get some answers.

8

THE POWER OF CHOICE

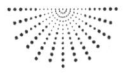

There was still a hint of orange in the sky to the west, behind the homes across the street from the house Tanner was in. The setting sun highlighted the homes' contours and cast long shadows. None of those shadows looked like a man holding a gun, so Tanner thought it a safe bet that they hadn't sent a man to hide across the street and snipe at him. Besides, he had seen their type before. They had triumphed over others so many times that they'd begun to think of themselves as invincible. It was one reason they'd adapted the flashy clothes and the cool car. They weren't all style and no substance; they just hadn't yet had the misfortune of running into someone who was better than them. Well, that was about to change.

Tanner zipped open the jacket on his jogging

outfit and tucked the gun in his waistband. When he opened the front door to go outside, he let the door swing wide then stepped into view with his hands held out by his sides. The men tensed for a moment but relaxed again when they saw that his hands were empty.

"Come on down the steps so we don't have to shout at each other," said the man who had spoken before. He appeared to be the mouthpiece for the trio.

Tanner came down the front porch steps and stood about fifteen feet away from them. The man who hadn't spoken was smirking. He was confident that they were in control.

The other man whistled loudly three times. It was a signal for the third man, the one who'd gone to guard the rear exit. He came around the side of the house and stood at Tanner's back, and about a dozen feet away. He was dressed like his friends and also had a shotgun within the folds of his coat. Tanner adjusted his stance so that he could keep all three of them in sight. It had the added advantage of turning him sideways, so that he presented a smaller target. Not that it would matter much given the weapons they had. With a flick of their wrists they could bring the shotguns up to fire. If hit with all three, there was a good chance that Tanner would be cut damn near in half. He used his head to gesture at the house.

"Are you responsible for that scene in there?" Tanner asked.

"Tinsley had it coming. Now, it's your turn."

"And what about his daughter, did she have it coming too?"

The man ignored the question and asked one of his own.

"Are you the dude that had a run-in with the people that were sent here before us?"

"Their names were Raúl and Felicia," Tanner said.

The man smiled. "Is that so? Well, let me introduce us. My name is Mr. Smith, the man on my right here is Mr. Jones, and the guy at your back is Mr. Johnson. What should we call you?"

"Sir will do."

Mr. Smith smiled. "Dude's got a set of balls on him, don't he, boys? It's too bad we'll probably have to cut them off to get him to tell us what we need to know."

"I was hoping you would be able to tell *me* something," Tanner said. "Raúl and Felicia didn't know much."

"What we know and what we don't know is none of your business. We want to know what *you* know. We were told that you were looking for the bastards that robbed that festival. Have you found them?"

"No."

"I don't know if I believe you. If you do know something, you're going to tell us where we can find them."

"I don't know where they are or even who they are. It sounds like you don't either. Too bad. That makes you worthless to me."

Mr. Smith huffed. "The balls on this dude." He looked past Tanner to catch the eye of his man, Mr. Johnson, then jerked his head to the right. He was telling Mr. Johnson to move away from Tanner and closer to himself and Mr. Jones. If they had to fire the shotguns, the way they were positioned, they might hit each other. Tanner adjusted his stance as the man moved. Once Mr. Johnson was standing to the right of Mr. Jones, Smith spoke to Tanner again.

"I don't think you know shit, but there's only one way to be sure."

"Are you asking me to pinky swear?"

Smith laughed. "Damn if I don't like you. It's too bad we're on different sides of this thing." Smith's face hardened and his voice lost all trace of humor. His tone was gruff when he next spoke, and his voice was a command.

"Put your hands in the air and turn around."

"No."

"You don't have a choice if you want to keep breathing."

"Yeah, I do," Tanner said. He pulled the gun from his waistband and fired three shots. The first round struck Mr. Johnson in the center of his forehead, the second entered Mr. Jones at a point between his eyes, and the third round ripped open Mr. Smith's throat. Once again, Tanner's speed and aim were remarkable. Not one of the three men had the time to even twitch in reaction.

The shots were still echoing in the air when Tanner moved past Mr. Smith. As he passed him, he looked down to see a pair of astonished eyes. Those eyes would soon close never to open again. Tanner's round had torn through Smith's jugular.

He stepped into the vintage Charger and backed it out of the driveway, to roar away down the street as the front doors of the neighbors opened up to see what all the noise had been about. Tanner took the first left, drove to the end of the block, and parked the car in front of a house that had a For Sale sign on the lawn. After wiping down any surfaces he had touched, he left the car unlocked and still running. He didn't care what happened to it.

In less than a minute he was back in the rented van and headed for home. He still had no idea of how to find the heist crew, and now he had killed three more of the people sent by whoever else was looking for them. Killing was how he made his living. He didn't like working for free.

Tanner drove along US-77. He needed more information. When an idea struck him as to where he might find it, he used the van's Bluetooth to make a call.

A familiar voice answered, saying, "Hello."

"It's me, Caleb."

"Hey, big brother! How is everybody doing there?"

"We're all good, and we're looking forward to seeing you again soon."

"I'll be there for Thanksgiving. I can't wait to see how much my niece and nephew have grown."

"Marian will be walking soon, and Lucas keeps asking me to let him ride a horse alone."

Caleb laughed. "Man, they're growing up quick."

"I called to pick your brain."

"About what?"

"Thieves."

"I do know a fair amount about that."

"I know, and maybe you can help me."

"I'll do my best," Caleb said.

Tanner went on to tell him about the heist crew that robbed the festival. Whether Caleb could help or not, it felt good to talk to his brother.

9

THE GERMAN

CALEB WAS A THIEF WHO WENT BY THE NAME OF Stark. Stark didn't pull heists, instead, he robbed other thieves to give them a taste of their own medicine. He was not well-liked among the larcenous class.

Caleb didn't know of the heist crew Tanner was looking for but said that he would ask his contacts about Marco Deering, the member of the crew that had been killed during the robbery. Regardless of the outcome he would get back to him.

One of Caleb's contacts was a fence who dealt in high-value loot. It was possible that he or one of his friends might have had business with Deering or the bearded man before.

Baby Marian was sleeping but Lucas was still awake when Cody returned home. He read to his son as he put him to bed, then joined Sara and Franny in the kitchen.

Franny had been with them for less than a year but was already one of the family. Cody liked her and loved how well she treated the children. Franny was the widow of a Marine who had died in action overseas. She didn't have children of her own.

Cody noticed that she was better dressed than she usually was for a night in and learned that she had just returned from going on a dinner date.

"With Crash?"

"I prefer to call him Raymond," Franny told him.

"I don't blame you," Cody said.

Franny called it a day a few minutes later and bid the Parkers goodnight as she went off to her room.

"Are you as surprised as I am that Crash and Franny are dating?" Sara said.

"I did notice them talking at the festival, but yeah, I didn't think Crash had the nerve to ask Franny out."

"He's got a lot to offer. He's smart, kind-hearted, and he's not hurting for money. I hope it works out for him and Franny."

"Time will tell," Cody said. His phone rang moments later. It was Kate Barlow.

"I hope I'm not calling too late, Tanner?"

"Not a problem. Were you able to blow up the still shots taken from the video?"

"Yes, and since I wasn't certain what was important and what wasn't I wound up having nearly a hundred of them. I've sent them in a zip file to the email address I have for you."

"I'll look them over tonight. Thank you, Kate."

"You're welcome, and I hope that they help."

Sara followed Cody into their home office and opened her laptop so that she could look at the photos too. She also suggested that they print them out using their photo printer. Kate Barlow had done a fine job of enlarging the masked men. Unfortunately, there was nothing in any of the photos to help identify them or point to where they might have gone.

Cody had been hoping to see a class ring or maybe a unique tattoo. All he saw was the hairy knuckles that Henry had said the driver of the van had.

Kate had also enlarged the bystanders who were standing near the barn when the robbery went down. Sara recognized a couple she knew.

"Elijah and Heidi were there when the shooting was going on."

"Let me see that," Cody said.

Sara passed him a photo that showed the couple crouched down behind a tree that was too narrow to shelter them. Elijah had his arms wrapped around

Heidi and was using his body as a shield in an effort to protect her.

"Here's another one showing them," Sara said. "Look at the man to the left of them. Does something look odd to you?"

Tanner took the new photo from her and scrutinized it. There was a man hiding behind another slim tree near Elijah and Heidi. Despite how grainy the quality was, Cody could see that the man was in his sixties. He was also dressed differently than everyone else around him.

"He's got a suit on."

"Yes," Sara said. "Who wears a suit to an outdoor festival in the country?"

"Are there any other photos showing him?"

Sara shuffled through the stack and found two more. She handed them to Cody. One photo showed Elijah and Heidi standing and looking relieved after Steve Mendez and Clay Milton had arrived on the scene. The man in the suit was at the edge of the photo and running toward the parking lot. The last photo showing him captured the man as he was opening the door of a white car. Even blown up you could barely make the man out, but the car appeared to be a luxury model. In the forefront of the photo was Mendez as he pulled a mask off one of the Carrawell brothers.

"This guy in the suit could be the buyer that

Tinsley was supposed to pass on the rare bill to," Cody said. "If I can find him, he might be able to tell me something."

"Finding him could be difficult," Sara said.

"Yeah, but it's a lead. I'll send these photos of him to Steve and see if he knows anything about him."

Sara yawned as she stood. "Are you going to be up late?"

"No. I'll come to bed soon."

Sara kissed him. "I'll read for a while after I shower. Don't be too long."

"I won't."

Steve Mendez did have news about the man in the suit. He told Cody that a man who fit his description and who drove a white luxury vehicle had skipped out of the hotel without checking out.

"The hotel still charged his credit card, but they reported that he left all his clothes and his shaving kit behind. That sounds like someone who wanted to put distance between himself and the town in a hurry."

"Did they have a record of what kind of car he was driving?"

"They had a plate number. I ran it and it came back as belonging to a Honda Civic. The name the guy gave them was a phony too. His address doesn't exist either."

"He must have been the man coming to claim the thousand-dollar bill."

"What are you talking about?" Mendez said.

Cody gave him the short version of what had happened the last few days. Mendez sighed.

"I didn't think this would turn out to be dangerous for you, Cody. Maybe you should let it go."

"I've never been known as a quitter. I'm also eager to get to the bottom of this now too. Don't worry, I can handle myself."

"Man oh man, is that ever an understatement, but be careful, and give me a holler if you need me."

"I'll do that."

Cody ended the call and headed off to bed. In the morning, he'd go looking for the man in the suit.

~

HE ATE BREAKFAST WITH HIS FAMILY AGAIN THEN headed off on foot to the small ranch office that was managed by Heidi Winhoffer. The young blonde was always in the office early and this morning was no exception. Cody exchanged greetings with her before showing her a photo of the man in the suit.

"He was near you and Elijah when the shooting was going on at the festival."

Heidi's pretty face formed into a scowl. "I

remember him. When he saw Elijah and I together he shook his head and sent us a dirty look. I think he's a racist."

Tanner nodded in understanding. Elijah was a light-skinned black man. He and Heidi had already had to deal with racism a few months earlier while at a concert in Culver. Two men had made stupid remarks as the couple were headed to Elijah's truck in the parking lot. Elijah ignored them until one of them made the mistake of grabbing Heidi by the arm. In the fight that followed, Elijah suffered a split lip. The two men didn't fare as well and spent the night in the hospital. Culver Chief of Police Brenda Harding, whose grandmother was black, hit the two with every charge she could think of.

"Did the man speak to you?"

Heidi shook her head. "Right after that the shooting started. If you want to talk to Elijah, he'll be here any minute. He's coming by to drop off the receipts for supplies he bought in town this morning."

Cody waited and Elijah appeared nine minutes later. When he saw Cody, he thrust out his hand while grinning.

"I was going to come by the house later to thank you for my promotion, Cody."

"You deserve it. But as much as I agree with it, it wasn't my idea, it was Rick's."

"I thanked him too, and I swear I'll do a good job and learn quickly. I already know a lot of what Rick does around here. I need to develop the people skills he has."

"That will come with time."

"Cody was asking me about that rude man we saw at the festival, Elijah. You know, the guy wearing the suit."

Elijah looked blank for a second, then he nodded. "Oh, that guy. Yeah, he looked at me like I was dirt or something. I think he was a damn Nazi."

Tanner cocked his head. "Why do you call him a Nazi?"

Elijah shrugged. "He was German, or at least, I heard him speaking German. He was mumbling to himself after the shooting stopped; it sounded like German to me. We had a neighbor who spoke it all the time when I was growing up, him I liked a lot."

"Why are you looking for this man, Cody?" Heidi asked.

"You know that I was a reserve police officer on the day of the festival, right?"

"Uh-huh," Heidi said.

"Chief Mendez thinks this man could aid in an investigation he's working on. When I saw that you two had been near him in the photo, I thought you might be able to help."

"Did we, help that is?" Heidi said.

Cody smiled at her. "Knowing that he's German might turn out to be important, so yeah, you helped."

Elijah thanked Cody again for his promotion and Cody left the couple to return to the house. He had no idea who the German was, but he knew someone who might be able to find him. He took out his phone and called Tim Jackson.

10

NO MORE GAMES

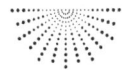

To say that Tim Jackson was a gifted hacker would be like saying that Leonardo Da Vinci had been good at painting. Jackson was levels above his peers, and it had gotten him into trouble with the mob when he inadvertently stole money from a corporation they controlled.

At that same time, Tanner was waging a war against the Conglomerate, which was what the mob was calling themselves during those years. Tanner convinced Tim to team up with him and the two of them brought down the Conglomerate and the man behind it, Frank Richards.

Tim and his wife, Madison, suffered more trouble recently that Tanner aided them in getting through. Tim was elated that he would get an opportunity to help repay Tanner for all he'd done for them.

"I've got the photos. Once I've identified what sort of car it is, I'll go about tracking it down."

"How will you do that?"

"It looks like a high-end auto. I'll bet you that it came loaded with extras, including a system that can track it in case of an emergency. Once I locate what system the manufacture uses, I'll take a peek at their info and find out where the car is and who the registered owner is."

"That sounds like it could take some time."

"The biggest hurdle is identifying the make, model, and year. There's software that can do that. Once I have that, I might have something for you in an hour or sooner."

"You're a wizard, Tim."

"Don't thank me yet. If it's a common car like a Lexus or a Mercedes, we might get dozens or even hundreds of matches. If that happens, then I'll have to look through each file and backtrack to see which vehicle had been in Stark, Texas on the day in question. Of course, that will only add a few minutes at most since the computer can do the search for me."

"How's Madison doing?"

"She's good, Tanner. She hasn't had a nightmare about her abduction in months now. She's downstairs in the hotel gym or I'd put her on to talk to you."

"Tell her that I said hello."

"I will."

~

TANNER'S ANNIHILATION OF THE TRIO WITH THE snake skinned boots had come to the attention of the people who had hired them to deal with him. They were an organization that Tanner had brushed up against once before in New York City. They called themselves Cipher.

Cipher was an entity with a reputation for getting the impossible done. Governments and even individuals with unlimited resources would contract with them to commit nefarious acts that couldn't be traced back to those requesting them. Cipher accomplished this by hiring a myriad of groups to do their bidding.

Tanner, Joe Pullo, and Jake Caliber the fifth had aided the authorities in thwarting a plan carried out by Cipher that would have destroyed the United States economy. Thanks to bribes and well-placed sources, Cipher was aware of their involvement. They were now beginning to wonder if the assassin Tanner was once again interfering in their business.

Two men and a woman met together in an office

tower in Dubai. One of the men was old, the other was thirty-five, and the woman's age was indeterminate. They had become aware that one of Cipher's money laundering endeavors had suffered problems. Like many problems, it seemed to be getting worse despite being given attention.

Raúl and Felicia had been reliable contractors for years, as were Mr. Smith, Mr. Jones, and Mr. Johnson. They had been bested by a man Felicia described as having, "Eyes that make one shiver."

The three members of Cipher realized that the description matched similar ones related to the American assassin, Tanner.

The old man suggested that they send another team of killers to Texas to deal with the problem. The younger man was willing to go along with that, but the woman protested.

"Remember what happened in New York City last year? We sat idle while assuming that the contractor we engaged would solve the problem. Instead, Tanner, Pullo, and Caliber destroyed the contractor's organization and ruined our plans. Our client was extremely unhappy, and I don't doubt it will be some time before they use us again, if ever. We cannot afford to let this… 'hit man' become a continuing thorn in our side. I say we quit playing games and destroy him now."

The old man considered her words as he took a

puff on his pipe. "Perhaps you're right. Who do you suggest we use?"

"Logan Fortunato."

The younger man chuckled. "Fortunato? To kill one man?"

The woman turned her cold gaze on her colleague. "Have you read the file we commissioned on Tanner?"

"No. What difference does that make?"

"Read it. It won't take you more than ten minutes. And I'll grant you that much of it was gathered through hearsay and speculation, but keep in mind that the accuracy of the information is said to be ninety percent."

The younger man picked up a computer tablet that was lying on the table before him. He accessed the correct file and began reading. Within a minute he licked his lips nervously. As he read deeper into the file, he was seen to swallow hard. As he was reaching the end of the report, his head shot up.

"He single-handedly destroyed Ordnance Inc.?"

"Yes," said the woman. "He fought a battle with hundreds of men and killed them all. Now do you see why I want to use Fortunato?"

"I do," said the man. "I now wonder if he'll be enough."

"Logan Fortunato and his people have never

failed," said the old man. "As remarkable as he is, Tanner is still just one man."

"Ordnance Inc. probably thought the same thing," the young man mumbled.

The woman smiled at his change in attitude. Minutes earlier he hadn't thought Tanner no more than a minor irritation, now he was worried. She had inherited her lofty position as had the younger man. She thought herself more worthy of the honor than he was. She had a steel spine and an innate understanding of what Cipher was and wasn't. She turned to her colleague and tried to make him understand.

"We have an advantage that Ordnance Inc., Alonzo Alvarado, and the others who have fallen to Tanner never had—we are anonymous. We are those who direct the chess pieces around the board, but we are never in jeopardy of being checkmated. Even if Tanner learned of our existence, he would have no way to find us. Cipher is no more than a rumor and we keep it that way by never personally getting our hands dirty."

"What if he knows about us already?" said the younger man. "Maybe that's why he's interfering in our business."

The woman shrugged her delicate shoulders. "The money laundering difficulty is an internal problem. That means we won't risk alienating a client again. If Fortunato fails and Tanner retrieves the rare bill before we do, it will be a loss, but not a devastating one. There are a world of mercenaries and paid killers we can throw at Tanner, and eventually they'll wear him down and defeat him, even if it takes decades. There is no way for him to track us down. Our triumph over him is inevitable. Now, let's move on to the contracts we're fulfilling in South America. How are they going?"

The old man opened a file in front of him to read aloud, and the meeting continued. To the heads of the organization known as Cipher, Tanner was a speed bump on an otherwise smooth and endless road of wealth and power.

TIM JACKSON CAME THROUGH ONCE AGAIN. He identified the white car belonging to the German as being a Volvo S90 Hybrid. There were thirty-two white S90s registered in Texas. After pinpointing exactly which one of those was in Stark, Texas on Saturday, Tim hacked into the files of the company that serviced the car's safety and security system. That allowed him to find out where it was currently located.

"That car is about forty miles north of Dallas,

Tanner. It looks like it hasn't moved in days. I'll send you the exact GPS location."

"You're the best, Tim. What's the name on the registration?"

"Karl Weber. That's Karl spelt with a K. I'll send you a copy of his driver's license photo."

"Do that, and thanks again."

"And I'll send you an alert if the car moves."

"It will probably move when I get there. Weber thinks he's safe, but if I can find him, so can others."

"Oh, so he's not a, um…"

"I'm not after him. I need him to tell me what information he has. Believe it or not, I'm helping the police solve a robbery."

Tim laughed. "I believe it. You're always full of surprises."

∽

Cody decided to fly to the Dallas area by using his own plane. He also made a stop at a neighbor's house to ask someone to come along with him.

Caroline looked surprised to see Cody on her doorstep, but she smiled and asked him to come inside. She was dressed in jeans and a flannel shirt and was carrying a pair of cotton gloves. Her long blonde hair was tied back in a loose ponytail and she wore no makeup. The natural beauty was still lovely.

"Cody. Hi. This is an unexpected pleasure."

"I hope I'm not bothering you or interrupting anything."

"No, I just came inside to get a drink of water. Daddy and I are doing a little late-season gardening."

"I'm actually here to see your father. I've a favor to ask of him."

"Follow me."

Caroline's home was no ranch, but it did sit on two acres. They were putting some of the land to good use by planting carrots, spinach, turnips, and what looked like collard greens.

Crash smiled wide and nodded enthusiastically when Cody said he needed a favor.

"Anything."

"I haven't asked yet."

"It doesn't matter," Crash said as he leaned over and pecked Caroline on the cheek. "You saved my baby. I'll always owe you for that."

"I want you to bring one of your drones and fly with me to the Dallas area. There's a man there I need to talk to. He might have information about the robbery of the Fall Festival."

"Why do you need a drone?" Caroline asked.

"I think there are other people looking for this man. I want to know if they're there already before I move in."

"Will Daddy be in any danger?"

"No. There's a chance that I'll face trouble, but I'll be ready for it. Your father will be piloting the drone from miles away. That will keep him safe. We'll stay in communication through equipment I have."

"I wish I could come with you," Caroline said, "but Jarod will be home from school before we could get back."

"Too bad," Cody said, and meant it. He liked Caroline. She could have also flown a second drone to give them more coverage.

"When are we leaving?" Crash asked.

"Come by the ranch as soon as you're ready. I'll be out at the hangar. It will take us over two hours to get there, and then we'll have to rent a car and drive the rest of the way."

"I should pack up food for you two," Caroline said.

"No need. Franny is already making sandwiches for the trip. We'll each have a thermos of coffee too."

"I like that woman," Crash said.

Cody nodded. "I hear that it's mutual."

~

THEY WERE READY TO GO AND ABOUT TO TAKE OFF when Cody saw a figure come running toward them across a field. It was Henry. He was wearing black jeans, black boots, and a bright blue hoodie that had the name and logo of his college on it.

He ran up to the plane and asked Cody where they were going. After Cody explained, Henry said that he wanted to come along.

"I thought you had an afternoon class today."

"It was cancelled. The professor is ill. I can send Grandma a text telling her where I'll be and I'm good to go."

"Climb on in," Cody said. Henry sat in the rear beside a backpack that was full of equipment, and soon they were off. Tanner had been right to think that someone else was looking for the German. That someone was named Logan Fortunato. He was planning to use the German as bait to catch Tanner and reel him in.

11

LITTLE MAN, BIG BRAIN

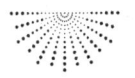

Logan Fortunato's real name was Larry Evers. Evers was physically unimpressive but had a high IQ and a devious mind. He stood only five foot four inches tall and weighed a hundred and thirty-six pounds. What he lacked in brawn he made up for in brains. He had learned to outsource his need for brawn while still a child in grade school.

Larry skipped grades in school, and thus was smaller than his classmates. He had been bullied by several kids in his class because of his size and intellect. When he grew tired of it, he decided to do something about it. That was when he made an offer to a kid named Bruce.

Bruce was Larry's opposite. He had brawn but was a dullard. While Larry was a nine-year-old who was much smaller than his twelve-year-old classmates, Bruce was the size of a high school senior. He was huge and had the strength to go with it. Despite being unable to do his assignments he was never left back or given bad marks.

No one teased the slow-witted Bruce, although to look at him you'd think he might be a prime target. The last kid who had called him a dummy wound up losing three front teeth from a single punch. This was before the days of zero tolerance toward violence. It hadn't hurt that the principal was afraid of getting on the bad side of Bruce's father. Young Bruce had come by his size honestly. Bruce Sr. was a hulking figure who it was rumored worked as an enforcer for a loan shark. The principal blamed the entire affair on the other student and had him suspended. Bruce was allowed to stay in school. The principal and Bruce's teachers were just waiting for the day when the boy would be moved on to the junior high where he would become someone else's problem.

Larry noticed all this and saw a way to use it to his advantage. He essentially hired Bruce. Hiring people was not a new experience for Larry. He ran a lawn business in the summer and a snow removal business in the winter and had been doing so since he was six. He realized that he didn't need to do work himself in order to have the work get done. With the help of his mother, his only parent, he hired older kids to cut lawns and shovel snow. The business was so successful that his mother was able to quit her "job" as a prostitute.

People were willing to work for money, and most people settled for less than they were worth. The difference between what Larry charged his customers and what he paid his workers was pure profit. He paid no taxes on that money and his only expenses were a pen and notebook to keep track of things.

To hire Bruce, he had to give the huge boy what he wanted most, and that was candy.

Bruce loved candy but never had the money to buy any. Larry kept Bruce supplied with sweets and Bruce made certain that Larry was never bothered again. Being profit minded, Larry thought of a way to make money with Bruce. In essence, he started a protection racket. Every kid in school had to hand over a quarter each Monday morning, or otherwise Larry would have Bruce make them sorry that they didn't.

It wasn't long before several parents complained. Despite his fear of Bruce's father, the principal was forced to call a meeting. Larry and his mother sat with Bruce and his father inside the principal's office to hear what had been alleged by several unnamed students.

Larry denied everything and asked the principal

what proof he had. Since none of the children were willing to step up and accuse Larry and Bruce personally, their parents had lodged the complaints. By doing so, they marked their children as snitches.

Larry stopped the protection racket. He'd already made more than enough to offset the cost of Bruce's candy addiction. Along with being smart, Larry was patient. He kept the names of the tattletales in the back of his mind and waited for summer to roll around.

Bruce wasn't the only big kid that he knew. There was a teenager named Victor who shoveled snow for Larry in the winter. Victor, who was fourteen, might have even been less intelligent than Bruce, but he was just as big, and he had a temper. During the previous winter, Victor had beat up a customer who had tried to get out of paying him for shoveling the man's walk. The customer claimed that Victor hadn't done a good enough job. Victor beat the man with his shovel and the cops were called. The man later refused to press charges. He didn't want the word getting out that he'd had his ass beat by a kid.

Victor wasn't into candy. What he wanted was a ten-speed bike. Larry agreed to get it if Victor did a few little favors for him. The four kids who had snitched on Larry all became victims of vicious beatings by someone wearing a mask. The fathers of those kids all left work the next day to find that the tires on their cars had been slashed and that their hubcaps and car stereos had been stolen.

Victor got his bike. Larry even added on a headlight because he was so pleased. Fencing the stereos and hubcaps covered the cost of the bike and left a few dollars for profit. The looks on the bruised faces of the kids who snitched was priceless.

When the new school year began, Larry's reputation as someone not to mess with was firmly established. As he got older, Larry retained the services of other Bruces and Victors for various projects. He made a business out of renting them out to those who needed muscle or used them to carry out plans he had made himself. He'd also come up with the name Logan Fortunato because he thought it conjured an image of a tall and muscular man.

In time, Larry, now Logan, saw the need to insulate himself from the risk of arrest or prosecution. That was when he hired a man named Hutchinson. Fortunato gave the orders and Hutchinson saw that they were carried out by their minions. At the age of forty-nine, Logan Fortunato was worth many millions of dollars and had never paid taxes or worked a day in his life. There was no record of him anywhere other than his school records. He didn't even have a birth certificate on file since his mother delivered him in the basement of a brothel with the help of a midwife. The birth certificate that was presented when he'd started school was a fake. As an adult, he'd never had a driver's license but had been chauffeured about most of his life. When he wanted a woman, he rented one. His utilities were listed under a false identity and he never used his real name. If the police ever came after him, they would assume that he was Hutchinson. Hutchinson knew that was a risk and Logan paid him to take it. Like the members of Cipher, Logan Fortunato had insulated himself well and was all but invisible.

He thought of himself as a director, an administrator. He told others what to do and they made certain that things got done. That freed up his time to pursue more cerebral pursuits. He spent a good portion of every day playing chess online.

When Cipher asked Logan Fortunato to handle the "Tanner problem," as they put it, Logan contacted Hutchinson by using a burner phone. As far as Cipher and other clients of Logan Fortunato knew, Hutchinson was Logan Fortunato. And for Hutchinson, Logan was just a voice on the phone.

~

"Tanner? *The* Tanner. This is that hit man we're talking about?" Hutchinson asked.

"That's him. They also sent me a file they had compiled on the man. He will be the greatest challenge we've ever had."

"Can I make a suggestion, Logan?"

"Yes."

"Tell Cipher no. I don't need to read a file to know what Tanner is. People have been trying to kill him for years and they all wind up dead. I don't know about you, but I don't want to join that list."

There was silence on the line. Then Logan said, "You're afraid of this man?"

"Yes. Yes, and I don't mind saying so."

"This sounds like you're talking from experience."

"I once worked for a man named Frank Richards. Richards was born wealthy and only got richer as the years went by. That wasn't enough for him. The man craved power so he made deals with the mob and eventually was on the precipice of controlling them. That was when he had a dispute with Tanner and decided to have him killed. Within weeks, Tanner had killed Richards and destroyed the organization he had built. Not long after that, Tanner went down to Mexico and killed a cartel leader who was living in a fortress surrounded by hundreds of guards."

"That was in the file I read, and yes, it's impressive, but the man relies on his brawn and guns to get things done. I can't imagine that I'll have trouble outwitting him."

"You might be right, but you can count me out."

"What are you saying?"

"I don't want anything to do with Tanner. If you're going after him, I won't be helping you."

"You truly are afraid of this man?"

"I am. I also don't plan to commit suicide by challenging him."

"Cipher is an important client. We make millions by servicing them and they're offering three times the usual fee for dealing with Tanner. If I refuse this contract the relationship we've built with them will be in jeopardy."

"Yeah, but you'll go on breathing. If you fail to kill Tanner, he'll kill you."

"Hutchinson, if you abandon me like this there will be consequences."

"I don't want to end our association but there are risks I won't take. If the police arrest me someday, I'll do time, but I'll still be alive. That's not true if Tanner gets me in his sights."

"Fine. Quit. But remember this, I'll make you pay a steep price for it."

Hutchinson laughed. "Logan, you won't be alive to follow through on the threat. Not if you insist on going up against Tanner."

"You're a coward!"

"A live coward. Goodbye, Logan. Remember that I warned you when Tanner catches up to you."

The line went dead and Logan looked at his phone with disbelief. He had never known Hutchinson to be rattled by anything.

"It doesn't matter," Logan said to himself. "I was prepared for this." By being prepared, he meant that he had a list of all the people they used. He also had a computer program that could make his voice sound exactly like that of Hutchinson. When he made the calls needed to assemble a small army to go after Tanner, the people he spoke to wouldn't know that it was he they were speaking with.

Despite his claim to Hutchinson that Tanner relied on brawn and guns, Logan's review of the file on Tanner revealed that the man was intelligent. Tanner was a thug, yes, but he was not a stupid one. The man thought things through and used surprise as his main weapon. To defeat him, one would be wise to turn that weapon against him.

Along with the report on Tanner, Cipher had also included a review of the problem with the missing rare bill and the search for the crew that stole the valuable old currency note. Logan was given the name and probable location of a man named Karl Weber. It just so happened that Fortunato knew of Weber and his association with Cipher. Weber was thought to be in hiding outside the Dallas area. Since

Tanner had been a step ahead of Cipher so far, it was a safe bet that Tanner had already gotten to Weber or was on his way to see him. It was a perfect opportunity to kill two birds with one stone. That is, if there was still time.

Fortunato stilled his mind and released the anger he was feeling toward Hutchinson. He did his best planning when he was calm.

Thinking of Karl Weber gave him an idea. Within ten minutes that notion blossomed into an ingenious plan that would bring about Tanner's death. Logan did a mental review of the resources available to him and smiled when he thought of a group of operatives he could use. They were seven of the best and were located in northwest Louisiana. If they were available, and hurried, they could make it to Weber in a matter of hours. Logan used a laptop computer to bring up the voice synthesizer that would help him mimic Hutchinson's deep voice, then he placed a call.

12

THE MAGNIFICENT SEVEN

Logan Fortunato contracted with a team of ex-special forces members to kill Tanner. He had used them a number of times in recent years and they had been excellent, professional, and well worth the high fee they charged. With the target being Tanner, Fortunato had to double that fee. The money was of little concern. Cipher covered expenses. They had never complained or questioned them because Logan had always gotten the results they wanted. He was determined that this time would be no different.

The team called themselves the Magnificent Seven. Not because of the movie that bore the title, but because they numbered seven and had a high opinion of themselves. They addressed each other by the code names they had used when they were in the military. Their leader was named Boss because he was in command. Boss was six-foot-three and hailed from Louisiana. The other six were named Gearhead, Rabbit, Turtle, Boomer, Biker, and Monkey. The names were given to them because they matched either their personalities or skill set.

Gearhead was into gadgets and had been working on cars as long as he could remember. His father owned an auto repair shop in Milwaukee. Rabbit was the smallest of the crew and the fastest. Turtle did everything slow including the way he talked. He was a black man with a southern drawl and sleepy eyes. People tended to underestimate him and usually regretted it—if they lived long enough.

Boomer was the team's sniper. Put him within a mile of a target and the target would soon cease to exist. He hailed from Alaska. When out of uniform, Biker wore leather, pants included. He had never owned or ridden a motorcycle. Monkey was given the name before joining the military. He had been a tree trimmer and could climb a tree like a chimp. It wasn't unusual to see him shooting at an enemy from the branch of an oak during a battle.

They worked well together and had been doing so for eight years in and out of the military. They had started their civilian lives by planning and executing armored car robberies with the same zeal and precision they once used to carry out missions against terrorists. After their fourth one, with the authorities turning up the heat, Boss decided they needed to end the robberies. They had grabbed enough money to live well but were too young to sit on a beach all day for the rest of their lives.

That was when they began selling their services and became involved with Logan Fortunato. Fortunato appreciated their talent and gave them targets that were worthy of them.

When Boss received the call asking him to go after Tanner, he said yes immediately. He and the others had heard of Tanner and knew that he was a formidable target. To sweeten the pot, Fortunato had information that might lead to Tanner's location.

Their mission had three objectives. They were to eliminate Tanner. That was priority one. Their second target was a man named Karl Weber. They were to interrogate him. It was possible that Weber could lead them to their third and final goal, the recovery of the rare bill and the elimination of the thieves who stole it.

Boss and his men were pumped and eager to complete every aspect of their mission. They were also aware that if Tanner was true to his rep, some of them might not survive. They knew this, but no one gave voice to it. The possibility of dying was something they had come to terms with a long time ago. Whether it came about through a man named Tanner, an IED, or God forbid, friendly fire, sudden death was just a fact of the life they led.

Boss and the others were on a helicopter forty-six minutes after accepting the mission. Their pilot was a man who would fly you anywhere at a moment's notice and ask no questions if you met his fee. Once you were on the ground, he would wait for you until the hour you stated that you would return. After that, you were on your own. Boss wisely always exaggerated his estimate of how long a mission would take, that way, their ride wouldn't fly off early and abandon them.

He was told that there was a likelihood that Tanner was looking for Karl Weber. If the assassin got to him first, he could have a huge lead on finding the thieves. If Tanner hadn't made contact with Weber, Boss would wait to see if Tanner showed up. That would be ideal and even better if they had the time to set up traps.

Boss's thoughts were interrupted by a voice coming over the headphones he wore. It was the pilot of the Sikorsky S-76.

"We'll be in the area in minutes. How far out do you want me to set down?"

"Do a flyover of the vicinity first and then we'll decide. But I'll probably want you no more than two klicks away."

"Roger that."

∼

Tanner, Henry, and Crash had landed at an airfield near Dallas then climbed into the rental car that was waiting for them. Karl Weber was on a farm fifty odd miles north of Dallas and near route 377. The cottage he had been in since fleeing the festival was surrounded by fields that had been harvested weeks earlier. He owned the twelve-hundred acres of farmland after inheriting it from a widowed sister who had passed away recently. The land was still registered in her name and he hoped that would be enough to keep anyone from finding him. It wasn't. Researchers working for Cipher had uncovered Weber's connection to the land. Tim Jackson had tracked Weber there by locating his car. Weber would have been better off if he'd stepped on the first bus or train he could find and riding it to its destination. It was too late for that now.

Tanner spent time checking out the area around the cottage with the aid of Crash's drone. The cottage was at the end of an area of cleared fields that had stretches of forests on either side of it, and a wider expanse beyond the cottage. A wooden water tower dominated the landscape as someone had painted it a bright yellow. The tower was facing the front of the cottage and was about a thousand yards away. Beyond it lay more fields. The cottage's nearest neighbor was miles to the north.

There were two vehicles parked on a paved section in front of the small home. One was Weber's white Volvo S90 and the other was a silver Toyota Camry.

While it was possible that the Camry belonged to someone sent to torture and kill Weber, Tanner doubted it. Crash had gotten his drone in low enough to make out details. There were small rainbow-colored teddy bears looking out of the car's rear window, and it had a vanity license plate that spelled the name Amelie. Tanner knew from the information Tim Jackson had supplied that Weber's daughter and only child was named Amelie. Why the man would invite his daughter to be near him when he thought people were out to kill him was beyond Tanner's understanding. The fool must believe that he had chosen the perfect place to hide. Tanner was soon to show him how wrong he was.

Tanner strapped on the backpack before heading on foot toward the cottage. Henry would accompany him while Crash stayed with the car and kept an eye out for trouble by using the drone. If anyone arrived in the area, Crash would warn them, and they could prepare. He was east of the cottage and the car they had arrived in was tucked beneath trees that were steadily dropping their leaves. There were still enough leaves left to place the car amid shadows.

Instead of cell phones or walkie-talkies they were using sophisticated earbuds that were hands-free and worked over a distance of five miles. Given the predominantly flat terrain they were on, that range might extend farther.

Tim Jackson wasn't the only one who had helped Tanner. Caleb had phoned while they were riding toward Weber's hideout and had news about the heist crew. The dead member of the crew, Marco Deering, had fenced several valuable pieces of jewelry in Las Vegas nine weeks before the robbery in Stark. The man who'd bought the items from him said that Deering was with a bearded man he introduced as his pen pal.

"Cody, that's pen as in the state pen. The bearded guy you're looking for might be an old cell mate of Deering's, or at least someone he'd served time with. I hope that helps."

"It does, Caleb. It narrows down the field. Did Deering ever mention the guy's name?"

"Yeah, the fence couldn't remember it, but he did say it was an uncommon name that started with a B."

"That narrows it even more. I'll tell Steve what you found and let him work on it. It might be enough to track the man down. Thanks, little brother."

"You got it, and stay safe."

"You too… Stark."

Caleb laughed. "I guess neither of us was cut out for the quiet life. Give Sara and the kids my love."

"Will do."

~

"What's in the backpack?" Henry asked Tanner. He was still wearing the blue hoodie that had his college's name and logo on it, but he was wearing it inside out so that the image and letters were difficult to make out and couldn't tie him to that institution and region of the state.

He and Tanner were walking toward the cottage to talk to Karl Weber. They were approaching it from the rear and moved slow enough to keep an eye out for boobytraps or anything that might warn Weber of their approach. Crash had been left with the car and had the keys for it. Tanner told him to leave the area if he felt threatened or if they lost contact for any reason.

"There's a chance that we might need more than our guns if someone else comes looking for Weber. The items in the backpack will give us an advantage."

"What have I missed since the other night?"

"After our talk with Raúl and Felicia I had a run-in with their replacements. They were a step up in the threat department. I doubt they'll be the last flunkies I'll have to deal with."

"Flunkies for who?"

"That's just one of the things I don't know. And I'm tired of not knowing things. Let's hope that Weber can supply some answers."

It was just good sense to assume that Weber would be armed. That meant that they couldn't just walk up to the door and knock. Tanner thought of a way to make Weber come to them.

~

KARL WEBER AND HIS DAUGHTER, AMELIE, WERE having coffee in the kitchen when a car alarm went off. It was Amelie's Toyota. Weber was tall and lanky, while Amelie was petite. Weber had been over forty when she was born and busy with his work. When his wife died, Amelie was raised by a series of housekeepers. As a result, the two had not been close, and Amelie had often acted out.

Weber was on his feet in an instant while reaching for the gun lying on the table. His breathing had sped up and his hands were shaking. He spoke to his daughter in German.

"Go to your room and be ready to climb out the window and run away if you hear voices."

"Papa, I can't leave you alone to face trouble."

"You must. If someone is here it will mean danger."

"That sounds like my car alarm. Maybe the wind set it off."

"Go Amelie. I'll see what it is."

Amelie went to the room she was using but stood in the doorway and watched her father. Weber crept toward the door with the gun held up in one hand. When he drew near to a window, he peeked outside and was relieved to see that there were only the two cars belonging to himself and his daughter.

He went from window to window and saw no one. As he was in the kitchen checking to see if anyone was at the rear of the house, he heard the car alarm shut off after running its course.

Amelie met him as he went back into the living room. She was smiling.

"See, I told you. It must have been the wind."

"It's not very windy."

"There have been a few gusts now and then."

Weber sighed as he felt the tension slip away. He tensed up again when the alarm began anew.

"Maybe I should park it along the side of the house, to cut down on the wind."

"Let me have your keys and I'll do it."

"No. You'll adjust my seat with those long legs of yours and I have it just the way I like it."

"All right, but I'll walk outside with you. I could use a little fresh air."

Amelie was fishing in her purse for her keys. She stopped what she was doing and looked up at her father.

"I'm sorry for what I've done. You're in trouble because of me."

"We are both to blame, Liebchen. I sealed my fate when I decided to work for the people who are after me now."

Amelie found her keys and they stepped outside onto the small porch. She used her key fob to shut off the alarm and the day was quiet once again. After she'd walked down the steps and onto the paved area in front of the home to move her car, Henry stood up from where he had been crouched behind the vehicle. He had given the car a good shove twice to activate the anti-theft sensors. They were designed to set off the alarm if there was enough vibration detected.

Amelie let out a short scream and dropped her keys. Her father was still holding his gun, which was a revolver. Before he could bring it up and take aim at Henry, he felt the barrel of Tanner's gun press against the back of his head. After making an incoherent sound of fright, Weber froze, and Tanner reached around him to take the gun away.

The older man looked as if he wanted to cry as he sank to his knees. He spoke to Tanner in a pleading tone with a German accent.

"I beg you. Let my daughter go. I will tell you everything, but she must not be harmed."

Tanner grabbed Weber and pulled him to his feet. "Get in the house and sit on the sofa. Your daughter too."

Henry was armed as well. Amelie followed his directions and walked back toward the house. As she was walking past Tanner, he reached out and took her by the arm as he stared at her. There was a familiar object in her blonde locks. It was a silver barrette in the shape of a heart. Tanner had found the young woman from Crash's earlier video that was taken the day of the robbery. That explained why Weber had allowed her to be near him. The people after him were the same people hunting her.

"I think your daughter will have more answers for me than you will, Weber. She was involved with the robbery."

Amelie's pretty face scrunched up as tears began to flow. "Are you going to hurt us?"

"No."

Weber spoke to his daughter in German. He was telling her that he would attack Tanner and give her a chance to escape.

Tanner spoke to Weber in German and told him that was a bad idea. He then switched back to English.

"I'm not here to hurt you or your daughter. I want the men who robbed the festival and to get back the rare bill they've stolen."

"You know about that?" Amelie said, as she dried her eyes.

"I do. I also know that the people your father was supposed to bring it to will do anything to get it back. They've killed several people already and I'm sure you two are next on their list. Tell me what you know, and I'll keep you safe."

Weber frowned as he took a seat on a sofa. "Why should we trust you?"

"I could make you talk by harming your daughter. Instead I'm offering you protection from the people who really want to hurt you. Think about that, Weber."

"He's right, Papa."

"Who do you work for?" Weber asked.

"I work for myself."

Weber looked at Henry. "And the boy?"

"He's not a boy. He may be young, but he can protect you too. But not here. Gather your things and come with us."

"What's your name?" Amelie asked, as she sat beside her father.

"I'm Tanner."

"Why do we have to leave here?" Weber asked.

Tanner was about to answer when he heard Crash's voice in his ear. The tech wizard was talking too loudly. Tanner saw Henry wince from the volume.

"Can you hear me?"

"I hear you, Crash. Talk in a normal voice."

Weber said, "Are you addressing me?" And Amelie gave Tanner an odd look. When he turned his head and pointed out the earbud he had, they nodded in understanding.

"Oh, sorry about shouting," Crash said. "I've got news. A helicopter just flew over the trees we're parked under. It was a big one, Tanner. You should hear it any second; it's headed your way."

"I hear it," Tanner said. The sound grew louder, then the air trembled as the helicopter lost altitude and the blades sent currents of increased air pressure toward the ground. Tanner went to a window and looked up. The chopper was hovering over the cottage at a height of less than two-hundred feet.

"Are they landing?" Henry asked. Tanner noted that his tone carried curiosity and not fear.

"I think they're just taking a look before they land, but they will land and then they'll come for Weber."

Henry moved over to the window on the other side of the door and squinted upward. "It's hard to tell from here, but I count at least four figures and the pilot."

"Yeah, but I'm guessing there's more. Whoever is behind this show will want to make certain that I don't keep getting in their way. They would send more than four," Tanner said. He shrugged off his backpack as he talked. He did not take his eyes off the helicopter other than to swivel his head for an instant to check his surroundings.

The helicopter rose up and veered away. It set down moments later near the bright yellow water tower that was west of the cottage.

"Why are they getting out so far away?" Henry asked.

"They're not. They're dropping off one man with a rifle. That water tower is only forty feet high, but it will give him a good view of the cottage and everything surrounding it. Once he's set, the others will move in. If they don't get us, the sniper will."

Amelie stood and gripped Tanner's arm. "Are you saying that we're trapped?"

He smiled at her. "That's their plan. I have a plan of my own."

"And what is this plan of yours," Weber asked.

"It's simple. I'm going to kill them all."

13

SMOKE 'EM IF YOU GOT 'EM

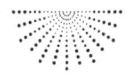

AFTER DROPPING BOOMER OFF AT THE WATER TOWER, Boss and the others in the helicopter rose up in the air again only to set down seconds later closer to the cottage. He'd looked through binoculars and had seen the teddy bears in the back of the Toyota. He felt reasonably sure that such a vehicle didn't belong to Tanner, and that meant that they had arrived before the hit man.

The Volvo belonged to Weber, Boss knew, and he had taken the shadowy figure he'd seen looking out a window to be the German. With Tanner nowhere in sight, grabbing Weber would be a piece of cake.

Boss was tempted to tell the pilot that he'd be back in a minute, but then remembered that the impatient bastard might take him literally and lift off sixty seconds later.

He told the pilot to head to the rendezvous point that was a short distance beyond the water tower and that they would meet up with him in an hour. He expected to be sending the chopper pilot off alone, and to tell him to stay on standby again. They weren't going anywhere until they were certain that Tanner wasn't coming.

Gearhead and Rabbit were on the move before the chopper even lifted off. Gearhead went left while Rabbit sprinted to the right. They were to circle around to a point a half mile beyond the cottage then head back. If Weber or whoever owned the Toyota tried to slip out the back and get away through the forest, Gearhead and Rabbit would run them down. Every member of the team was wearing a bulletproof vest and everyone but Boomer was armed with a Glock as a sidearm and an AR-15. Boomer's rifle of choice was a Barrett with a special scope. He also preferred to carry a SIG Sauer P-210 with a walnut grip instead of a Glock. Every member of the team was dressed in black from head to toe.

Boss was pumped. They could grab Weber and make him talk, kill the bastard, then lay in wait for Tanner to appear. Boss's good mood faded along with those plans when he saw something fly out an open window of the cottage. The object was followed by another, then two more. They were smoke grenades. The advantage Boomer's sniper rifle had given them had just been nullified. As good as he was, Boomer couldn't hit what he couldn't see.

Karl Weber was a sixty-six-year-old ex-banker. He was not throwing smoke grenades. Tanner was on site, and Boss knew he was in for the fight of his life. He keyed his earpiece.

"Look alive. Tanner is here."

∼

TANNER WATCHED BOSS AND HIS REMAINING MEN approach the cottage after seeing Gearhead and Rabbit run off in opposite directions. He assumed that they'd been sent off into the trees to circle around and come up behind him.

He'd sent Henry out the back door and into the trees with Weber and Amelie while the chopper was landing at the water tower. Henry was to get the father and daughter to the car where Crash was waiting and to get out of the area. Henry had protested. He'd wanted to stay and fight. Tanner insisted that he go with Crash and the others.

"If they're attacked, they'll need you."

Henry nodded as he looked down at the floor. "And you don't need me."

Tanner had laid a hand on his shoulder. "I need you to protect them. Will you do that?"

Henry looked up and nodded. "I'll keep everyone

safe. Be careful, Tanner."

As he watched Gearhead and Rabbit, Tanner thought that Henry's head start should be enough to keep the men from catching up to him. Doubt crept in as he saw how swiftly Rabbit moved among the trees.

The kid will be all right, Tanner thought. *He's got what it takes.*

Turning his mind to dealing with the remaining four men converging on him, Tanner lobbed the smoke grenades out the window. They would send up a wall of smoke that would block the sniper's view of the cottage and the immediate area in front of it, at least for a little while. It would be time enough for Tanner to leave the cottage unseen and get to work killing the men who had arrived in the helicopter.

Tanner reached into the backpack and brought out a pair of thermal imaging goggles. After strapping them on, he tested them and found that they worked. Not much of the smoke had come in through the window, so he turned off the goggles and moved about the cottage. Smoke or not, there was a chance that the men attacking would fire on the house. They had little to lose by doing so and there was always the chance that a stray round might find a target. It was safer to leave the cottage through the rear and circle around. As he entered the bedroom that was being used by Amelie, Tanner used the same window that Weber had wanted Amelie to climb out of earlier. Tanner stepped outside and into the smoke, where he activated the goggles again. Moving quietly, he eased toward the front of the cottage until he was crouched behind Weber's Volvo. Tanner scanned the smoke for heat signatures and saw one the size of a man moving toward him.

~

Boss was impressed with Tanner's tactics but was not unprepared. He didn't have a pair of goggles, but he did have a rifle scope that could detect thermal images. It was in a supply pack and something that he hadn't expected to need until nightfall. He wished he'd had the foresight to give it to Boomer before leaving him at the tower but on a clear, crisp autumn day it hadn't crossed his mind.

Monkey was loaded down with the supply pack. Boss thought he was behind him and on his right but couldn't see him because of the smoke.

He whispered, "Monkey?"

"Here, Boss," came a reply from nearby. Boss

moved in the direction of the voice and saw a shape form amid the thick smoke, then another one a few feet behind it. The first shape turned out to be Monkey. Boss noticed that his eyes were reddened from the smoke. His eyes felt fine, but the smoke was giving him a tickle in his throat.

"Monk, I need you to run the pack out to Boomer on that water tower. There's an infrared scope in there."

Monkey squinted toward the direction of the cottage. "I want to stay here and hunt down Tanner. This smoke can't last forever."

"Boomer can finish this quicker than we could if he had that scope."

Boomer keyed his mic and spoke to Boss. He was having the same thoughts. "I can't make out shit. Have Rabbit run that thermal scope out to me."

"Negative. Rabbit is busy hunting possible runners. I'm sending Monkey."

"Make it quick. I can kill Tanner and anyone else from up here. Send me that scope and don't forget to activate your IR flashers. We don't need to have any accidents."

Boss sent Monkey off toward the water tower and smiled. Once Boomer had that scope it would enable him to counteract the smoke and beat Tanner at his own game. He keyed his mic and told Turtle and Biker to stay put. There was no sense in their wandering around when they couldn't see three feet in front of them. He also told his men to activate their IR flashers. The team wore them on the front and back of their belts. Once Boomer had the infrared scope, he'd be able to identify them by the infrared flashes the small devices emitted. Those red flashes were invisible to the naked eye but plainly seen through the scope.

A sudden gust of wind swept in and dispersed some of the smoke. Boss hoped it would allow Boomer to acquire a target even without the special optics. No sooner did he have that thought when he heard the hiss of another smoke grenade go off. The sound had come from nearby. He froze in place and looked about intently. He hoped to catch a glimpse of Tanner amid the smoke and got his wish.

The vague shape he'd seen standing behind Monkey hadn't been Turtle or Biker. It had been Tanner listening in on his conversation with Boomer.

Boss had heard of how unique and intense Tanner's eyes were. Although he was standing face-to-face with the man, he still couldn't see his eyes. They were covered by the goggles he wore.

Boss was bringing up his AR when he felt three distinct blows hammer into his chest. He was wearing level 4 body armor beneath his shirt. It stopped the rounds from penetrating but did nothing to keep away the pain of impact that knocked him on his ass.

Boss felt like he'd been hit by a car and was having trouble taking a full breath. The pain was incredible, but it only increased when something hard struck his left knee and made him scream.

He heard Turtle and Biker calling to him but was unable to respond. Agony had him clenching his teeth and he wondered what had happened to his rifle.

A shot rang out. It was followed by the sound of a body hitting the ground. The smoke was wispier near the ground. When Boss turned his head, he could see that the body that had fallen near him was dressed in black leather. He also saw the neat entry wound between Biker's eyes. Then, a string of shots erupted. It was Turtle firing on full auto. One magazine was spent, then two, then three. Despite the pain fogging his mind, Boss wondered if Turtle had known that he was on the ground and beneath the bullets' path, or had he just panicked and shot off the rounds blindly. No. Turtle wouldn't panic, and he wouldn't have risked killing a brother. He had taken a calculated risk.

Booted feet came toward Boss. A moment later and Turtle's face came into view as he leaned over and spoke to Boss in his distinctive drawl.

"Are you wounded?"

"I hurt like hell and the bastard smashed my knee with something, but my vest stopped the rounds."

Turtle smiled, slowly, the way he did everything. "I think I got him."

"Have you seen his body?"

"Not with all this smoke floating around, but I heard someone grunt and a body hit the ground. I emptied a magazine in that direction after that."

"Help me up."

Boomer's voice came over their ear mics. "Boss, give me a sitrep. What was all that shooting?"

Boss touched his earbud to key his mic and answered. "Turtle has killed or wounded Tanner. And… Biker is dead."

"Fuck!"

"Yeah."

"Monkey is climbing up the ladder now. I'll be switching scopes as soon as he hands it to me."

"Turtle and I will head toward the water tower. Monkey?"

"Yeah, Boss?"

"Go to the chopper and tell the pilot to fly in here."

"Copy," Monkey said.

"You and Turtle keep your flashers hot, Boss," Boomer said. "I'm going to put ragged holes into anyone who's not the two of you."

"I copy that," Boss said, and touched his mic to turn it off.

Turtle had an arm around him and was helping him to hobble along. He spotted something lying in the grass and pointed at it. "What's that?"

Turtle leaned over and picked the object up. It was the infrared goggles Tanner had been using. Their black casing had taken a round and both lenses were shattered. Boss noticed that the head and chin straps were still fastened.

"You must have shot those off of Tanner's head, and maybe put one in his brain too."

Turtle looked around warily, but the smoke was still preventing him from seeing more than a few feet. "Let's get out of this smoke."

It occurred to Boss that he wasn't certain of what direction they were going. "Are you sure we're headed toward the water tower, Turtle?"

Turtle stopped walking. When Boss turned his head to look at him, he saw the tip of the knife that was sticking out of his throat. Turtle's body collapsed a moment later and dragged Boss down with him. He had barely hit the ground when he felt his earbud being yanked away, followed by his sidearm. Then he watched as Tanner removed Turtle's gun belt and strapped it on. The IR flashers were on that belt.

As for Turtle, true to his nature, he would die

slowly. The wound to his throat had also severed his spine. He lay on his back with a stunned expression on his face.

Boss finally got a look at Tanner's eyes. They were as advertised, and he wondered what it was about them that made him look so damn menacing. There were red welts on Tanner's forehead and chin caused by the goggles being forced off him by Turtle's round. Tanner reached down and yanked Boss to his feet. It was only then that Boss saw that more of Turtle's bullets had made contact. The shirt Tanner wore had two round holes on the left side of his chest. Only Tanner was wearing a vest too.

"Let's go."

Boss glared at him. "Where?"

"To that water tower. We're expected."

Boss looked down and realized what Tanner was up to. Boomer would be viewing the world through the infrared scope. The two of them would look like a pair of glowing blobs, and with Turtle's belt flashing, Tanner would appear to be a friendly until he cleared the smoke and could shoot at the water tower.

Boss shook his head. "No sir. No way! I won't help you kill my friend."

Tanner raised Boss's gun and brought it down along the side of his head. "I don't need your help."

Boss grunted and collapsed again. Tanner used

zip ties to bind his wrists and ankles. He winced from the pain Turtle's two rounds had left him with. He also had one hell of a sore neck. The bullet that ripped the goggles off had wrenched his head around with unnatural speed. One of the slugs that hit him in the chest had come close to missing the armor plating. If it had, his degree of pain would be at a whole other level. If he still lived.

Tanner keyed his hands-free mic by saying the word, "Connect," When he heard a click, he spoke to Henry. "Are you back at the car yet?"

Henry's voice filled his ear, and it was obvious that he was running. "There are two guys chasing us, and man is one of them fast."

Tanner left Boss and took off running toward the direction Henry had taken earlier. He was past the cottage and had just missed running into the side of it because of the smoke he had let loose. The smoke dissipated as he entered the trees. Tanner heard Henry speak to Weber.

"You and your daughter keep running hard. We have to make it across this clearing and into those trees."

"Henry! What's going on?"

"They're gaining on us."

"Where are you?"

"We're heading southeast and away from the car. I didn't want to lead them right to Crash."

Tanner ran as hard as he could, knowing that he had a lot of distance to make up. He left the trees and entered a clearing. Far ahead he saw two figures running. One was faster than the other and nearly across the wide clearing. Entering the trees on the other side were three figures he took to be Henry, Weber, and Amelie.

Henry spoke while running. His pounding feet made his voice uneven, but Tanner noted that there was no trace of fear in his tone.

"I've got an idea that might work. I won't be able to talk for a minute while I try it."

"Crash?"

"Yes, Tanner?"

"Use your drone to keep an eye on Henry. If you see anyone headed your way, just get in the car and drive out of here."

"I can't leave you two without a ride."

"You can and you will. Henry and I can handle ourselves."

"The drone is in the air, but I still have to locate him among the trees."

"Henry?"

"Yeah."

"I'm on my way."

"Okay, but I have to be quiet now."

"Stay safe, boy. I'm coming."

Tanner was sprinting across the clearing. His

pace faltered when he heard the sound of gunfire being exchanged, then he kept going.

When Crash's whispered words of, "Oh no," came through the earpiece, Tanner dreaded to know what he was seeing through the camera on his drone.

"What's happened, Crash? Do you see Henry?"

"Tanner... I think Henry is dead."

14

WORTHY

Henry had been pushing Weber and Amelie to move faster when he'd looked over his shoulder and saw the two men rushing toward them across the open fields that lay between two patches of forest. It was Gearhead and Rabbit. Rabbit was far out in front of his partner and eating up the ground at a terrific pace.

"Head to the left," Henry told Weber. Judging by the speed of the men chasing them, they'd never make it to the car in time to drive away. As part of their due diligence, he and Tanner had set up traps that would have worked to injure the men chasing him. Henry couldn't put them to use. If they continued in that direction, his companions might set them off inadvertently and there was no time to stop and explain the danger to them.

The old man, Weber, was wheezing but his long legs made up for his lack of fitness. Amelie, although young and vibrant, was barely keeping pace with her father. Henry glanced over his shoulder again and cursed when he saw that the men had gained more ground, especially the fast one. As if that wasn't bad enough, the outline of a third man was visible off in the distance and was coming on strong. If he'd been on his own, Henry might have outrun Rabbit or made it back to the car with enough time to drive away. He wasn't alone, and he had promised Tanner that he would protect Weber and Amelie.

The thought occurred to Henry that the new man he'd seen in the distance might be Tanner, but he couldn't count on that. He had to prepare himself to face off against three men, and all of them armed.

He needed to do something, and he couldn't risk getting Weber or Amelie injured. Ahead, at the edge of the clearing, he saw the mouth of a trail that led off into the forest. Henry headed for it with the hope of losing his pursuers among the trees. It seemed unlikely as the trees were spaced wide apart from each other and offered little in the way of concealment.

Earlier, when Tanner's voice had come through the earbud, it gave Henry hope that he was nearby. But then Tanner asked him where he was, and

Henry knew he was on his own. He told himself that it would be all right, that he could handle himself. All he needed was a plan.

The trail made a sharp left behind a short hill. Before rounding the curve, Henry looked back once again. The second man following them seemed to be slowing down, but not the first man, he'd catch up to them soon. Henry knew the only reason the man wasn't firing on them was that they wanted to take Weber alive so they could question him. They couldn't risk killing their only lead to find the robbers.

Rounding the curve behind the hill, Henry saw a small clearing ahead where there was an old shack missing its front door and leaning precariously. It looked as if the next strong wind would blow it down. Beyond the shack the trail curved around another hill. A plan formed in Henry's mind in an instant. It would either work or seal his fate. That was when he ended his conversation with Tanner and told Weber and Amelie to continue on without him.

His mentor's last words to him were to stay safe, and to assure him that he was coming to his aid. Rabbit would catch up to him in a matter of seconds. It was up to Henry to survive on his own.

He slowed as he reached the old shack and ran

toward it instead of staying on the trail with Weber and Amelie. He ran behind the dilapidated structure an instant before Rabbit rounded the last bend.

~

Rabbit's legs were moving like pistons as he strove to catch up to his quarry. He smiled as he came around a curve on the trail and saw that Weber and Amelie were beginning to slow as they ran out of steam.

But where is the guy in the hoodie?

Rabbit was passing the shack when Henry darted out from his place of hiding and tackled him to the ground. The impact was jarring, and Rabbit felt a sharp pain in his lower back as he landed atop the rifle that was hanging by its strap.

He overlooked the pain and reached for the gun on his hip with one hand while his other arm was busy shielding his head from the blows Henry was raining down on him with the rock he was holding. The gun slid free of its holster, but Rabbit never got the chance to fire it. Henry had smashed the rock against the side of his head and put his lights out.

~

TO SERVE AND PROTECT

Gearhead wouldn't win any races, but he was in excellent condition. He knew that he could certainly outlast an old man, a kid, and a girl. And of course, Rabbit had to show off and speed ahead of him to get to them first.

He'd heard the conversation between Boss and Boomer and knew that Biker was dead. It didn't seem possible. He'd known Biker since Parris Island. The man was more of a brother to him than the ones who shared his flesh and blood. It also sounded like Turtle might have killed Tanner. If the bastard was still alive, Boomer would get him, and if Boomer didn't kill the hit man then Gearhead swore to himself that he would do it.

Gearhead rounded a curve along the trail and saw a shack up ahead. Rabbit had caught up to the kid in the blue hoodie and was tussling with him on the ground. Rabbit was lying on his side with the kid on top of him, and there was something in the boy's hand.

Is that a gun?

Rabbit was holding a weapon, but the kid had hold of his hand and was preventing him from aiming the barrel at him.

Gearhead had gotten closer, and yeah, the kid had a gun and he was pointing it at Rabbit. Gearhead slid to a stop, swung his rifle around, and took careful aim. Three rounds perforated the hoodie. One of them struck the hood itself and turned the blue color of the cloth into a deep red. Gearhead released a sigh of relief as the body tumbled to the dirt. The form lying sideways turned over and fired at him. An instant before the slug that ended his life found its way into his brain, Gearhead realized that he'd been horribly mistaken. It hadn't been Rabbit who was lying on the ground. It was the boy. And that must mean...

Gearhead died knowing that he had just killed his friend.

~

AFTER KNOCKING OUT RABBIT WITH THE ROCK, HENRY leapt up and peeled off his hoodie. He then removed the black, long-sleeved T-shirt that Rabbit was wearing and put it on. The shirt was clammy with Rabbit's sweat, but Henry didn't notice, he was busy staring at the bend in the road. Gearhead had been slower, but he wasn't that far behind and would arrive at any second. And after him would be the third man he'd seen. Fearing he didn't have enough time to wriggle Rabbit into his hoodie, Henry put the hood over the man's head and let the garment drape across his back. If he set the scene right, Gearhead wouldn't notice the discrepancy and would only see that his friend was in trouble and fighting for his life. The plan had worked. Gearhead and Rabbit were dead, but a third man was on the way. Henry lay on the ground with a gun in his hand and waited to ambush while playing dead.

～

WHEN CRASH'S DRONE LOOKED DOWN ON THE SCENE seconds later, he saw what appeared to be three dead men. The huge bloody stain covering the back of Henry's hood made tears appear in the older man's eyes.

～

CRASH'S DESCRIPTION OF THE SITE OF THE GUN BATTLE caused Tanner's breath to catch in his throat. He came around the bend in the trail and took in the bodies, but his mind didn't want to accept what he was seeing, and he held out hope that Henry might still be alive. He was moving toward Henry to check his condition when he registered that the hoodie was only draped across the body. Despite the angst and dread he was feeling his expertise had not abandoned him. He'd been trained by Spenser Hawke to observe and not merely see… and something was not quite right.

"Tanner."

Tanner heard someone call his name then saw the head on one of the "bodies" lift its face from the ground. It was Henry.

Crash's voice filled Tanner's ear. He was still looking down on them by using the camera on his drone. "Look out! One of those guys is alive."

"It's okay, Crash. It's Henry."

"Henry?" There was a buzzing sound as the drone was brought lower to get a better look. Crash laughed when he saw Henry wave to the drone. "Oh, thank God."

"See if you can track down Weber and his daughter, Crash. I doubt they have the stamina to have gone much farther."

"You got it, Tanner. And Henry, don't scare an old man like that."

As Tanner walked toward Henry, he took in the scene and understood what had happened. Henry had used guile to outwit the men pursuing him. He had kept his wits about him and defeated men who no doubt had ten times his experience.

Henry walked up to him while peeling off Rabbit's clammy shirt. Beneath it he wore a plain white T-shirt.

"What about the others?" Henry asked.

"Two are dead with three more remaining. One

of those is injured and out of the fight. Tell me what happened here."

Henry did so, and it was as Tanner had intuited from viewing the scene. With pride showing in his eyes, Tanner placed a hand on Henry's shoulder and said one word.

"Outstanding."

Henry beamed at the praise.

∼

THE SMOKE HAD CLEARED TO REVEAL THE DEAD BODIES of Biker and Turtle, along with the bound form of Boss. Without his earpiece he couldn't communicate, nor could he answer his phone with his hands behind his back. Rabbit and Gearhead weren't responding either.

Monkey had been talking to the helicopter pilot when he heard from Boomer and learned what was happening. Monkey got the pilot to agree to land near the cottage so that he could grab up Boss and get out of there. Boomer would stay on the water tower and keep watch for Tanner while Monkey rescued their commander. They didn't doubt that Boss had been left there as part of a trap, but Tanner didn't know Boomer. The instant he showed himself, Boomer would put him down. And besides, they weren't about to abandon Boss or leave until they knew what had happened to Rabbit and Gearhead.

~

Monkey leapt from the chopper before the skids had touched the ground and rushed over to Boss.

"Where's Tanner?"

"He was communicating with someone and took off running."

"And now Rabbit and Gearhead aren't answering their coms."

"Shit."

Monkey had the zip ties cut in seconds and handed Boss his sidearm. They were moving toward the helicopter with Boss still limping and needing support.

"Let me have your earpiece, Monk."

Monkey handed over the earbud and Boss activated it. "Boomer?"

"Here."

"Tanner may be listening, switch to the backup frequency."

"Roger."

Boss switched the frequency on his earpiece as well. Boomer made contact seconds later and Boss responded.

"Do you see anything, Boomer?"

"Negative."

"Keep watch. We're coming to you now."

"Copy that."

Monkey helped Boss onto the helicopter and climbed in. The pilot lifted off and headed to the water tower, where they landed without incident. Monkey jumped from the helicopter and kept watch for trouble while Boomer made his way back down the ladder on the tower. He leapt the final eight feet and joined Boss in the helicopter, then was followed by Monkey.

Boss put on a pair of headphones and spoke to the pilot. "Fly east. We need to find two of our men."

As the helicopter began to rise, the pilot told Boss that he was getting close to his departure time and that if he wanted him to stay longer, he would need more money. Boss resisted the urge to shoot the man and agreed to pay.

Someone saved him the bullet. A rifle round pierced the chopper's windshield and struck the pilot in the chest. The helicopter was sixty-two feet in the air when the wounded pilot released the collective. The metal bird lost altitude instantly. Before it hit the ground, the pilot made a desperate grab for the collective, but in his wounded state he only managed to push the control downward. The helicopter hit the ground with great force, it did so hard enough to break off the tail rotor and send the body of the craft flipping over twice. The pilot was ejected during one of those flips.

~

THE FIRST THING BOSS BECAME AWARE OF WHEN HE regained his senses was smoke and knew there was a fire burning somewhere in the wreckage. Looking around, he saw Monkey. The man's head was sitting at an angle that it was never designed to attain.

Boomer was alive and bleeding from a leg wound. Boss called to him. "This thing is on fire; we've got to get out of here."

Boomer opened his mouth to answer but never got the chance. A bullet had passed between his parted lips and blew out the back of his head. Boss had no idea what had happened to the gun Monkey had given him. When he reached for it, he found an empty holster. He was about to make a grab for Monkey's rifle when Tanner spoke to him.

"If you want to live, tell me who hired you?"

"Go fuck yourself, Tanner."

Tanner reached into the wreckage and grabbed Monkey's rifle. He then claimed the SIG Sauer in Boomer's holster.

"Who hired you?" he asked Boss.

"I told you to go fuck yourself. Now, if you're going to kill me, then kill me."

"I don't have to kill you. You'll soon burn to death."

Boss jolted at those words. And yes, the smoke had increased. It was coming from somewhere behind or beneath him.

Tanner pointed at Boss's left hand. "You don't feel the pain yet, do you?"

Boss looked down and saw that three of his fingers were missing.

"You'll feel the flames when they get you."

"I'm still not talking. You're wasting your time."

"We'll see," Tanner said. He took several steps back as the smoke increased. Boss might die of smoke inhalation before the fire reached him. It soon became apparent that the flames could affect him without touching him, as the surface he was resting on became hot. Whatever the material was, some sort of plastic, it began to change shape as it softened. Boss tried to free himself from his harness and found that it was damaged. He kept a knife on his belt and reached for it to cut himself free. But the knife was on his left side, and with his missing fingers, he couldn't grip the hilt.

Tanner shouted to him. "Give me the name of the man who hired you and I'll get you out of there."

"Fuck... you. Arrgh!"

Boss was in agony, but he still refused to talk.

"A name!"

Boss spoke through teeth that were clenched together in pain. "No."

Tanner raised his rifle and shot the man, ending his misery. Whatever else Boss had been, he had the grit to not give in under extreme pressure. Tanner had to admire that. Unfortunately, he still had no idea who was sending people to kill him. Maybe Weber or his daughter could shed some light on that. They were with Henry again and waiting near the cottage for him. Tanner had told Crash to take the rental and head back to the city. He didn't want Weber or Amelie to know of his involvement if they didn't have to. He also told Crash that he and Henry might be staying in Dallas overnight. He asked Crash if he wanted to take a flight home or stay at a hotel and meet up with them the next day. Crash said that he would stay at a hotel so that they could all fly back together.

"And call me if you need me," Crash said.

Tanner said he would and thanked him for his help. The older man was really growing on him and his drones were a handy tool to have.

~

TANNER TURNED AWAY FROM THE BURNING helicopter when he heard a moan come from a clump of weeds on his left. It was the helicopter pilot. The man was still alive.

Both of his legs were broken, and blood seeped from the chest wound Tanner had given him. When Tanner walked over to look down at him, he spoke with a raspy voice.

"I'll take the deal."

"Deal?"

The man moaned in pain while balling up his fists, then spoke in a weaker voice. "Logan Fortunato. That's the name you want. He hired this crew. Now, call an ambulance for me."

"The smoke from the crashed helicopter will bring the authorities out here."

"Oh yeah. I didn't have to tell you shit, did I?"

Tanner pointed his gun at him. "And I don't have to keep you alive."

"Wait! I can tell you how to find Fortunato."

"Why would you know that?"

Another jolt of agony gripped the man. When it passed, he attempted a smile that made him look insane. "I knew Fortunato before he started using that name. His real name is Hutchinson, Guy Hutchinson."

"Who does he work for?"

The man winced, then said, "Don't know."

"If you're lying about this, I'll find you."

"I ain't lying. And I never liked Hutchinson, the smug bastard, so do to him what you will."

Tanner took off running for the cottage. Someone would be coming to investigate the smoke and they had to be out of the area before that happened.

Logan Fortunato. That's who wanted him dead. Now all Tanner had to do was find out why.

15

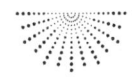

PHASE TWO

"I've never heard of Logan Fortunato or Guy Hutchinson," Karl Weber said. "The organization I've been working for calls themselves Cipher."

"I've heard of it," Tanner said.

Tanner had driven Weber's Volvo away from the cottage and into Dallas. After abandoning the car, Tanner, Henry, Weber, and Amelie climbed into a taxi and took it to a hotel. Tanner spoke with Weber and Amelie while Henry kept an eye out for trouble in the lobby. The car was left in a tow-away zone to get rid of it. Weber wouldn't be using it again, not after Tanner told him that tracing the car was how he had tracked him down.

Tanner had already heard part of Amelie's story as they drove to the city. She had fallen in love with the ex-con, Marco Deering, and made the mistake of telling him that her father often bought and sold valuable items for wealthy clients. Amelie was so enraptured with Deering that she allowed him to talk her into robbing her father. Now that they were safe inside the hotel room, Tanner got the details from Amelie.

"Marco said that whatever he and his friends took from Papa wouldn't be his personal property and that an insurance company would reimburse his client. I finally gave in and started spying on Papa for him."

"Do you live with your father?"

"No, but I still have a key to his apartment from when I did live there. I used it to sneak in and go through his things."

Amelie found out that her father was going to Stark to meet with Alex Tinsley and purchase the rare 1880 bill. When Marco learned the value of the old currency, he put together a crew and went after it. They had no idea that Amelie's father was connected to Cipher or that they would face competition from other thieves. Weapons that had been brought along to intimidate were used in a firefight that left Marco Deering dead.

Instead of being wanted on robbery allegations the remaining members of the heist crew faced charges of murder and were being hunted by people working for Cipher. Amelie said that they became aware of how serious things were when they had trouble fencing the rare bill. They were told that it was too hot to handle and that there were people other than the police looking for them, dangerous people.

Tanner had received a text from Steve Mendez on the drive into Dallas. The chief told him that none of Marco Deering's known prison associates had an unusual first name that began with B. There was a Bob, two Bills, and a Brian.

When Tanner asked Amelie about it, she explained. "Marco's friend is named Bohdan, Bohdan Kushnir."

"They were in prison together?"

"Yes and no."

"What does that mean?"

"Bohdan worked in the prison as a guard. He was fired and spent time in jail when the warden found out he was selling drugs and access to cell phones."

"This Bohdan, does he have a beard?"

"Yes."

"And who was the man who drove the van?"

"His name is Gage Kline." Amelie made a face. "I don't like him. I once saw him kick a dog for no reason."

"And the last man's name?"

"Cory Sparks. He's Bohdan's nephew and is about my age."

"Where can I find them?"

"I don't know. When Bohdan realized there were people after us, he said it would be best if we all split up. I was living with Marco in his apartment, and since he was... after the robbery, I thought it was best not to go back there or the police might find me and question me."

"You were right. And then what did you do?"

"I called Daddy and asked if I could stay with him. I also told him the whole story. I screwed up so bad, Mr. Tanner. I betrayed my father and now we have people who want to kill us."

Tanner stood to walk over to the room's small desk, but paused to massage his neck, which was still sore. He also had a wide bruise forming on his chest from where Turtle's slugs slammed into the bulletproof vest he was wearing. Once he was at the desk, he grabbed the hotel stationary and a pen, then handed them to Amelie.

"Take this into the bedroom and think about everything you know about Bohdan Kushnir, Gage Kline, and Cory Sparks. As you do that, I want you to write down what you know. No detail is too small. Write down things they said about their lives, childhood, what their favorite foods are, what they drink, the names of women they might have mentioned, anything. Write it all down."

"Okay. But why do I have to go into the bedroom to do that?"

"It's quieter in there and it will be easier for you to concentrate."

"Oh, okay." Amelie stood, but before walking down a short hallway to her bedroom, she looked back at Tanner. "Your friend saved our lives. I thought for sure that those men were going to catch us. Please thank him again for me."

"I will."

"And thank you too."

When Amelie was in the bedroom, Weber shook his head as he stared at the closed door.

"She's so different."

"Your daughter is different, how?"

"Amelie went through a rebellious streak in her teens and got into trouble. She had also been abducted by a kidnapper, but the FBI killed the man and rescued her. And now this new trouble with these thieves… it's changed her. She's much nicer, more respectful, and more caring than she used to be."

"How old is she?"

"Twenty."

"Maybe she's growing up."

Weber nodded, then he asked Tanner a question.

"You gave her that task to do because you want to speak to me alone, yes?"

"Yeah, but she might also think of something that will help me find those men. I also want to find the people behind Cipher."

"I can't help you. I've never met with them, and I've only interacted with people like myself, men and women who are cogs in the machine they've built. One definition for the word cipher means nobody, a nonentity. That is what Cipher is. They exist only as an idea and never get involved other than to issue orders anonymously."

"How did you get tangled up with them?"

Weber sighed. "Getting involved with Cipher was not my first foray into criminal activity. When I was a banker, I laundered money for certain, extreme organizations."

"Neo-Nazi organizations?"

Weber blinked in surprise. "Yes, that's true. Why did you assume that, because I'm German?"

Tanner had guessed correctly because of what Elijah and Heidi had told him about Weber's reaction to seeing them together at the festival. There was no reason for Weber to know about that.

"It was a lucky guess. Continue your story."

"I was questioned as part of an investigation and was facing the possibility of serving many years behind bars if convicted. That was when I received a phone call from a man who said he could help me. The government had an informant who could testify against myself and three others. Once I agreed that I would accept the caller's help in return for doing certain favors, the informant was killed in police custody."

"How long ago was this?"

"That was twenty-eight years ago and happened in Berlin."

Tanner's jaw clenched. He'd assumed that Cipher was a new organization. They weren't. They were international, had been around for decades, and were only now becoming a rumor. That was quite an accomplishment. It made him realize how formidable the people behind everything that had happened were.

"What are your plans, Weber? You must have known that you couldn't hide out on that farm forever."

"Documents are being made that will give Amelie and myself new identities. They should be ready sometime tomorrow and I will receive a call to come get them. I'm not a complete fool, Tanner. I saw this day coming for one reason or another. I have funds that I can access and a place to go to." Weber released a small moan. "I never thought I would be leaving with Amelie at my side. What will her life be like now?"

"At least she's alive. Alex Tinsley's daughter was

murdered and the men that did it made him watch her die."

Weber looked as if he might be sick, but he composed himself after swallowing hard several times. "You and that boy saved us. I am in your debt, Tanner."

Tanner nodded. "I know of a way you can pay us back."

～

AFTER BEING UNABLE TO MAKE CONTACT WITH THEM, Logan Fortunato realized that Boss and his men had failed. It was unfortunate but not unexpected given Tanner's reputation. It also meant that Tanner had Karl Weber. And Tanner was actively working on finding the crew that stole the rare bill. In time, Tanner would be closing in on them as well.

Fortunato smiled. A lesser man would consider the current circumstances and think that all was lost. On the contrary, things were moving along nicely. Let Tanner win the battles; Fortunato would win the war.

He knew from perusing the file on Tanner that the hit man wouldn't be satisfied with having survived an attack. No. He would want to know who was behind it and seek revenge. That meant that there would be another opportunity to kill him.

Fortunato was inside his office at his estate. It was actually a working farm. He liked being surrounded by nature but did none of the actual work himself. His food was cooked for him by a chef, his house cleaned by a maid, and on those rare occasions when he ventured away from his home, he hired a limousine.

The outside of the home looked like a typical farmhouse as did most of the interior. Fortunato's office was different. It was a room where he spent most of his time and he had it decorated in fine style with art on the walls and a collection of books on science, history, and biographies.

No one else was allowed in the room and he had both a thumbprint and a retina scanner integrated into the security system. If by some miracle someone who wished him harm discovered where he lived, his office would double as a safe room. In the center of the room was a table that held an antique chess set. That table could be slid aside to reveal an escape tunnel. The tunnel led to an outbuilding where there was a car. He hadn't driven since he was a teenager but was sure that he still possessed enough skill to do so, especially if his life were on the line.

While leaning back in his favorite chair, Fortunato pondered his next move. He needed to destroy Tanner, but he couldn't risk the loss of more valuable assets like Boss and his team.

Tanner had triumphed over a pair of interrogators, then killed a team of three men who by all accounts were deadly. Fortunato knew that Boss and crew had been lethal, but the seven men met their superior in the assassin.

Fortunato smiled again. Tanner would be expecting to face a greater threat. So why not give him one? He would send a small army at the man, but they would not be people whose loss would be missed. Yes, give the hit man what he expects and see if he can handle it. Judging by the past, Tanner would triumph. That's fine, because it will set him up for what will come after that.

Boss and his team had simply been Phase One. There would be a Phase Two and a Phase Three. Fortunato was a chess player. He knew it was worth the sacrifice of any number of pawns in order to allow your queen to be placed in a position where she could checkmate the opponent's king. He would send those pawns against Tanner. But, who to send?

The truth was that he had no pawns. Knights, bishops, rooks, yes, but no pawns. However, he did once have dealings with a group that he'd classified as such. They were a motorcycle gang that lived outside the small town of Pachaw, Texas. They called themselves the Diablo's Doubles and their leader was a man named Hombre.

Fortunato had hired them to do a bit of dirty work for a client about a year earlier. They had been successful but in a crude manner. They had eliminated the target and his security. That was fine, but afterwards they had proceeded to gang rape the target's wife and daughter before killing them too. That sort of unpleasantness tended to make the police take a personal interest in a case. It also risked leaving behind DNA evidence that could have led to arrests and convictions. If that had happened, Hombre would have brought up his name in a bid to get a lighter sentence. The police knew nothing about him, and Fortunato wanted to keep it that way. The whole affair with the biker gang had left a sour taste in Fortunato's mouth. He had decided to never use the lowlifes ever again—until now.

Tanner would be expecting an increase in numbers or skill level. Diablo's Doubles weren't a step up in class over Boss and his men, but there were certainly a lot of them. If the club's membership number had stayed the same, Tanner would be going up against at least eighteen men. That would keep the hit man busy. And who knows, maybe Hombre or one of his men would get lucky.

If luck was on their side and they killed Tanner, Fortunato would give them another assignment.

They could track down and kill Guy Hutchinson for abandoning Fortunato at such a crucial moment. He would tell the bikers to be especially cruel and to make sure the man suffered horribly.

With his decision made, Fortunato went online to play chess. There was a woman in Argentina who had proven to be a worthy opponent and he enjoyed playing her.

It was just a matter of time until Tanner surfaced again. When he did so, Diablo's Doubles would get a call.

16

WE'RE IN THE MONEY

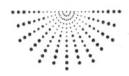

Tanner and Henry took turns guarding Weber and his daughter until Weber received the call to come and pick up his new ID.

His contact lived in a house in the Oak Lawn section of Dallas. It was a quiet neighborhood with nice homes. Tanner and Henry accompanied Weber to the Tudor style house but stayed outside while the deal was done. When Weber returned, he and Amelie had new identification, including passports. Amelie was frowning.

"I've always loved my name. I don't want to be someone else."

"You'll get used to it," Tanner said. He'd had to change his name when he was sixteen and lived under numerous aliases for years. Nearly a quarter of a century passed before he was able to claim his name again, along with his land and legacy.

Weber asked Tanner to drop him and Amelie off at the bus station on Lamar Street. He didn't mention their destination and Tanner didn't ask. He had requested that the man do him a favor as repayment for saving his life. Weber assured Tanner that he would do as he asked.

Amelie had compiled the list that Tanner had asked her for. She had scribbled down a list of things she knew about the men involved in the robbery. Tanner had glanced over it and thought that much of it was useless—such as the fact that Bohdan Kushnir liked mushroom soup—but he also thought there might be a few things that could turn out to be valuable. One in particular could lead to him finding, Gage Kline, the bastard in the van who had nearly run over Henry.

Tanner sent Weber and Amelie a nod when they were parting and received one back from Weber. That wasn't good enough for Amelie. She stood on her tiptoes and kissed first Tanner, then Henry on the lips. Tanner noticed that Henry blushed a bit. Although he wasn't a virgin, the kid was still just seventeen, and Amelie was a very beautiful young woman.

"Thank you for saving us," Amelie said.

Tanner noticed Weber's hesitation to leave. "Is

something wrong?"

"That farm we were at. It's quite a valuable piece of land. It is a shame I didn't have time to liquidate it and move the money into an account under my new identity."

"Walk away from it. If you attempt to keep it or sell it, Cipher might use it to track you down someday."

Weber sighed. "It is such a waste."

"Let's go, Papa," Amelie said, as she took her father's hand. Tanner and Henry watched as they walked into the bus station as the first step toward their new lives.

~

Crash met with them at the airfield. He had decided to stay overnight and fly back home with Tanner and Henry. He was waiting outside the hangar.

When he saw Henry, he gave him a playful punch on the arm. "You scared the hell out of me yesterday. I really thought that something serious had happened to you."

"That was the whole point," Henry said, "But it was only meant to fool the men who were chasing us."

"Did you find out what you needed to know,

Cody?" Crash asked.

"Not all of it, but we're one step closer. And that drone of yours was a big help."

Crash grinned. "Good. I told Lannie what happened, and she said that she was glad she didn't come. It would have scared her to see you facing off against so many men."

"They won't be the last ones, not until I find the thieves and that rare bill."

"I'm not worried about you. Hell, you're Tanner Seven, and you've got Eight here watching your back."

"Eight?" Henry said.

"Yeah, you'll be Tanner Eight someday. If there were ever any doubts you dispelled them yesterday."

Henry shook his head. "I'm a long way from getting that title."

"Maybe so, but Henry, I've studied top assassins for decades, and the Tanners in particular. Kid, you've got what it takes to be one. You not only defeated the men who were after you, but you protected the people who were with you. Cody chose well when he picked you to be his apprentice. And hey, I can't wait to start collecting souvenirs when you get the title. I've collected items related to every Tanner."

"That reminds me," Tanner said. "I've got something for your collection. I figured it would be a good way to repay you for your help." He reached into the backpack he was carrying and removed the damaged thermal goggles. They had been destroyed by one of the .223 rounds Turtle had fired from his AR-15, and the slug was still embedded in them. Tanner's neck continued to be sore from having his head jerked around as the goggles were ripped off by the force of the bullet.

Crash grinned down at the goggles, then looked up suddenly. "Were you wearing these when the bullet struck them."

"Yeah."

"Damn. That was a close call, Cody."

"A man named Turtle did what's called spray and pray when he fired his rifle on full auto. His prayer was nearly answered."

"Turtle? Why was he named that?"

"I don't know, but he did seem to talk slow."

Crash admired the goggles again. They were now useless junk to Cody, but a treasure to Crash. He held up the goggles.

"This is going into my collection. Thanks."

"You're welcome. Now, let's get back home."

∽

They landed on the ranch in the early afternoon to find Caroline and Sara waiting for them along with Henry's grandmother, Laura. Cody had called and told them what time to expect them. Sara had brought along their dog, Lucky. The black Labrador practically tackled Cody over his exuberance at seeing him.

Laura and Henry went home to the house they rented on the ranch and Crash showed off his souvenir to Caroline. Both she and Sara looked worried.

"That bullet came awfully close to hitting you," Sara said.

"But it still missed," Cody said. He didn't mention the two that had hit him in the vest. Sara would become aware of the bruise left behind soon enough.

Crash and Caroline headed for home in her blue SUV while Cody drove his pickup truck and followed Sara to the house with Lucky riding beside him.

Both of the children were taking naps with Franny keeping an eye on them. Over a cup of coffee in the office, Cody told Sara about what had happened in Dallas.

"Did you give the names of those three men to Steve?"

"Yeah, but I'm going to track them down. Even if he caught them and put them in jail, the people who want them dead would make certain they got out on bail so they could kill them."

"When are you going to look for them?"

"Early tomorrow, very early, and Henry and I will be heading out to the desert too. Cipher, through their lackey, Fortunato, will be sending another group after me. I want to deal with them in a place of my own choosing."

"How will you lure them to the desert?"

"Karl Weber is going to make contact with someone he knows is connected to Cipher. He says that they've been friendly but that he expects the man will sell him out, either for a reward or out of fear. Once that happens, Cipher will send people, and I'm expecting that it will be more than before."

Sara's expression turned angry. "Steve asked some favor of you."

"He had no way of knowing that it would have turned into this. I was just looking for a group of heisters for him. I'm still looking for them."

"You make sure you're ready for what they send at you."

"I'll be ready, more than ready. If I had any doubts, I wouldn't involve Henry. Then again, he needs to be involved. It's a good way for him to learn."

"How did he do in Dallas?"

Cody smiled and told her about Henry's trick with the hoodie.

Sara laughed. "That sounds like something you

would have thought of doing."

"I've done similar things in the past. He's going to make a great Tanner someday."

"You've had less strenuous contracts to fulfill. Is there anything I can do to help you with this?"

"Now that you mention it…"

~

AMELIE HAD RECALLED THAT ONE OF THE HEIST CREW, Cory Sparks, had a dog, a pointer, named Jolene. It was the same dog that the van driver, Gage Kline, had kicked for no reason. Amelie said that Cory loved the dog and that he had placed it in a kennel when they knew they had to run. If Sparks loved the dog, he would check on her by calling the kennel often. If they could figure out what kennel the dog was in, Tanner could have Kate Barlow or Tim Jackson hack into their phone's account and find out what number he called from, and where the phone was located.

Sara volunteered to make the calls while Cody spent time with the children once they woke up from their naps. By dinnertime, she was still at it.

"I've spoken to just about every kennel in the state and there's still no pointer named Jolene, but I'll keep searching after dinner if you'll keep watching the kids."

"It's a deal. And thanks for doing this."

"Thank me when I find that dog," Sara said.

~

She disappeared into the office after eating to make more calls. Cody had been about to text her to come and kiss Lucas goodnight when Sara entered her son's bedroom with a big smile on her face.

"It took over two hundred calls, but I've found the dog."

"Great. What's the name of the kennel and where is it located?"

"The dog isn't at a kennel. I called every kennel in the state and came up empty, then I remembered that Lucky's groomer also offers boarding for pets. The dog is at a grooming shop named Petsense. It's in Laredo."

~

Tanner and Henry left the ranch early and drove to Laredo. Tim Jackson had come through again and found out that Cory Sparks called the grooming shop from a burner phone. Realizing that it wouldn't help Tanner to know that, Tim hacked into the grooming shop's computer and studied the files with their customer information. Cory Sparks had recently changed his emergency contact to a phone number that matched the burner phone number. He had also stated that he would be staying with a friend at a marina, in slip 129. This had been written down as a notation by whoever had taken in the dog. Tanner was thankful for their thoroughness and Sparks' big mouth.

Breaking into a boat is nowhere near as easy as breaking into a house. The house doesn't rock when you move around on it. Tanner left Henry to stand watch and took his time easing onto the vessel. He didn't want to wake Cory Sparks and have to face a desperate armed man. He wanted to wake him up to a nightmare that would increase his sense of desperation.

Sparks believed there were people out to kill him. Tanner would take advantage of that belief and use it to his advantage.

~

SPARKS WAS ONLY TWO YEARS OLDER THAN HENRY, but he was pudgy and looked as if he were rarely out in the sun. The flab around his middle was easy to see as he was sleeping in only a pair of white boxer shorts. Instead of keeping the cabin dark, Sparks had a lamp set on low. Tanner had searched the small boat and confirmed that Sparks was alone onboard.

Tanner had been hoping to find Sparks' uncle, Bohdan Kushnir, on the boat as well. It didn't matter. Not if he could get Sparks to tell him where his uncle might be.

Tanner slapped the teen awake then covered his mouth with a gloved hand. Sparks woke and tried to sit up. His hand reached for the weapon he'd left on the nightstand, but it was no longer there. His struggles ended when he realized that Tanner's gun was pointed at his face.

"If you make too much noise, I'll kill you right now. Do you understand me?"

Sparks didn't respond. His eyes were locked on that deadly little black hole at the end of Tanner's gun.

Tanner removed his hand from his mouth only long enough to slap him again, but harder. Sparks blinked away tears and stared up at Tanner.

"Are you going to be quiet when I remove my hand from your mouth?"

This time Sparks nodded, so Tanner eased his hand away. Sparks asked a question.

"How did you find me?"

"Your uncle ratted on you."

"Bohdan? He would never do that."

"He held out for a little while, but there's only so much pain a man can take."

Sparks' pale skin grew whiter. "Is he dead?"

"Forget that. Where did you put the rare bill you and your partners stole?"

"What? Bohdan has it."

"It wasn't with him when we caught up to him. Where would he have hidden it?"

"It should be in his truck."

"A pickup truck?"

"No. Bohdan has an old Peterbilt. He's a truck driver. Well, whenever the damn truck isn't broken down, he is. He told me when we split up that he would be staying in his truck until things cooled down. It's got a sleeper cab. I figured that was where you found him."

"Is the truck broken down now?"

"Yeah, it was. But Bohdan said he was going to get the cranking system fixed now that he had some money. Maybe it's running."

"Where is the truck parked?"

"It's at that big truck stop in Dilley, on Highway 35."

"Describe the truck in detail."

Sparks did as Tanner ordered and then asked a question.

"If Bohdan wasn't in the truck, then, where was he?"

Tanner pressed his gun against the side of Sparks' head. "I ask the questions. You give the answers. Got it?"

"Yes. Yes, sir."

"Where can I find Gage Kline?"

Sparks made a face of displeasure that reminded Tanner of the one Amelie had made when he'd mentioned Kline.

"I don't know where he is or care, but I hope you find him and hurt him bad."

"I plan to kill him."

"Shit. Did you kill my uncle?"

"No."

"Are you going to kill me?"

"If I do, you'll be the first to know."

Tanner left Sparks tied up and gagged before heading to the small city of Dilley with Henry. He'd text Steve Mendez and tell him where the kid could be found. Tanner was betting that the weapon Sparks had on his nightstand would match one of the guns fired at the festival. It would tie him to the robbery and the killing of Marco Deering.

Tanner found Bohdan's truck without much difficulty. It was a Peterbilt 379 that looked like it had seen several million miles and had received little in the way of TLC. It was no wonder it broke down often. Sneaking up on Bohdan Kushnir was even more difficult than surprising his nephew had been.

A truck, like a boat, rocked when someone climbed onto it.

Henry stood nearby to keep an eye out for witnesses. Although the sun had yet to come up, the truck stop was active. Most of the activity was taking place by the restaurant but the fuel pumps were working, and one trucker had been pulling his rig out to get an early start when they had arrived. There were three other trucks parked near Kushnir's. They all had out of state tags and looked at least a decade newer than Kushnir's ancient truck.

Once Tanner had picked the lock on the door, he opened it and moved swiftly into the sleeper cab where the bearded ex-prison guard was stretched out on his back. Kushnir didn't so much as twitch when Tanner pressed a hand over his mouth. Tanner was wondering if he were dead when he realized how strong the odor of whiskey was within the cab.

Kushnir wasn't asleep and he hadn't been murdered. He was so drunk that he had passed out. Tanner removed his hand from Kushnir's face and turned on the light inside the small compartment. There were three empty liquor bottles on the floor and a fourth bottle that was nearly empty. A stain was near one of the bottles. It looked as if Kushnir had vomited at some point. He also hadn't bathed in some time.

The rare bill was inside the blue gym bag that

had been used on the day of the robbery. There were no workout togs in there, but there were the empty wallets, rings, and other jewelry that had been stripped off the people who'd been inside the barn on the day the festival was robbed. Kushnir must have had enough sense to get rid of the cell phones so they couldn't be traced. At the bottom of the bag were the old comics, stamps, and baseball cards that had been stolen from the booths. A bank's night deposit bag held what was left of the money taken from the festival. Along with the amount of cash Tanner had gotten from Cory Sparks, it looked like he had recovered most of the money taken. Gage Klein would have the rest.

Tanner studied the valuable currency through its protective, clear vinyl case and was impressed with how little wear and tear the bill had suffered after being around over a hundred and forty years.

On the dashboard was a cell phone and a receipt from the truck stop's garage. The problem with the charging system had been fixed. The eighteen-wheeler had a new alternator and a new battery. That was good. It meant that the truck should run. Tanner secured Kushnir with zip ties then left the truck to speak to Henry.

"Bohdan Kushnir is dead to the world from having drank too much."

"Did you find the bill?"

"Yeah."

"So, what's next, call Chief Mendez?"

"If I do that the local cops will be sent to investigate and they might get the credit for recovering the bill. It would be better if Steve got the credit, so I'm going to drive the truck back to Stark. You can follow me in the pickup."

Henry looked up at the massive old truck. "You can drive that thing?"

"Yeah, and I'll teach you how to do so someday too, along with operating heavy machinery. Although, the new trucks have automatic transmissions."

"That's still a lot of machine to move around."

"The hard part is backing them up. Go get the pickup and come back here, then follow me to Stark. We'll be home in time for lunch."

~

THE OLD PETERBILT WAS SLUGGISH. THE TRAILER swayed some because it was empty, and the day was windy. Tanner was glad for the breeze and kept the windows open halfway despite there being a nip in the air. It helped to dispel the stink of the booze, vomit, and body odor. They arrived back at the Stark town limits after making one stop for a bathroom break and coffee. Kushnir never stirred but only mumbled in his sleep once.

Steve Mendez met them at an old abandoned train yard. He wrinkled his nose in disgust when he looked in on Kushnir but laughed when he saw the gifts Tanner had brought him.

"The victims will be damn glad to get their wallets and jewelry back. These bastards even took people's wedding rings."

Tanner held up the rare bill. "I'm not an expert in the law, but since this was used for money laundering shouldn't you be able to confiscate it?"

"It's possible."

"This thing is valuable, Steve. If sold at auction, I'm betting your department would clear over a million dollars. That would help Clay when he becomes chief and will ease your budget worries when you become mayor."

"Holy crap, Cody. You're right. I never thought of that. This disaster is starting to look like a blessing, thanks to you."

"Did anyone pick up Sparks in Laredo yet?"

"Yeah, and I'm waiting on the ballistic results."

"Kushnir's rifle is on the floor of the cab. You'll find the magazine in the glove box."

"What would you have done if you were pulled over by a cop on the way back here?"

Tanner smiled. "I would have told him that I

worked for you as a deputy."

"Hell, I wish you did. The crime rate would be zero."

"Yeah, but you'd have to triple the size of the morgue."

~

Tanner joined Henry in the pickup truck. They were headed back to the ranch.

"Any idea where we might find the last guy?" Henry asked. "I owe that bastard for almost running me down. And the son of a bitch was actually trying to kill that little girl."

"His name is Gage Kline. And no, I don't know where to find him yet. Amelie said that he once mentioned he was from Chicago. It's possible he ran back there to hide."

"I hope not. I'd love to get my hands on him."

"Maybe we'll find out something while we're in the desert tomorrow."

"I'm looking forward to that. I want to see what preparations you make to deal with what will be a massive attack."

"That reminds me. I want you to stop in town today and buy fishhooks and fishing line. We'll need them in the desert."

"Fishhooks? In the desert?"

"They're part of the preparations we're making."

Henry laughed. "I can't wait to see what that's all about."

~

Henry was to be dropped off first before Cody returned home. When they arrived at the house Henry shared with his grandmother, Henry found that he had a visitor. It was twelve-year-old Chrissy Kyle. The girl had ridden her bike for miles to come see Henry.

Cody watched from the window of his truck as the little girl walked over to Henry as he got out. Chrissy had been talking to Henry's grandmother, Laura. She had stopped by to thank Henry for saving her and she had a gift for him.

"A pair of fuzzy dice?" Henry said.

Chrissy pointed at Henry's 1980 Z28 Camaro. "They're for your car. Aren't classic cars supposed to have them?"

Henry looked down at the girl and smiled. She had her red hair tied back in pigtails and looked adorable.

"Thank you, Chrissy. I'll hang them from the mirror."

"Cool."

Henry looked over at her bike. It was a pink

three-speed. "How far did you ride to get here?"

"We live on Sycamore Street, in that new development."

"What? That's got to be about twelve miles from here. Why didn't you ask someone to give you a ride?"

Chrissy looked down. "Daddy wouldn't have brought me here. I don't think he likes you."

Henry started to say that the feeling was mutual, but instead he asked Chrissy how her wrist was doing.

"I'm all better, well, almost."

"Let me give you a ride home. I'll put your bike in my trunk and you can hang the dice on the mirror."

Chrissy shook her head. "If Daddy saw me getting out of your car, he'd go bananas."

"Then I'll drop you off a couple of blocks from your home, but I'm not letting you ride all that way back to your house. It's too far."

Chrissy smiled. "Thank you, Henry."

Henry drove off a few minutes later with Chrissy sitting beside him. The pair of red fuzzy dice were hanging from the rearview mirror.

Laura called to Cody. "That little girl has such a crush on him."

Cody nodded. "That's for sure." He told Laura goodbye and drove to the ranch house. As he did so, he wondered what Cipher would throw at him next.

17
VULTURE BAIT

THE LEADER OF THE DIABLO'S DOUBLES WAS NAMED Hombre. Hombre had been burned in a fire during a run-in his gang had several years ago with Jake Caliber the fifth. Hombre had been left bald, scarred horribly from the burns, and speaking with a raspy voice.

Hombre and a dozen other men had faced off against a lone Jake Caliber and were defeated, with most of them killed. Now, he was preparing to go up against Tanner. The man had not learned a simple lesson—superior numbers do not guarantee a victory.

TANNER AND HENRY WERE IN THE CHIHUAHUAN Desert, about an hour's drive from El Paso, Texas. Weber had come through for Tanner by contacting an acquaintance he knew was connected to Cipher. He had asked the friend for help and told him that he was hiding out in the desert. The location he mentioned was the spot where Tanner and Henry had been busy laying traps. The first one was crude but effective, the second was designed to be used against a foe that numbered many.

Now that he had recovered the rare bill and helped Mendez, Tanner had turned his focus on finding and killing the people who had been trying to kill him. While that included the people behind Cipher, he didn't expect to find them. According to everything he had learned about them, Cipher's members were untouchable because they were anonymous. He didn't intend to spend time searching for them, a task that might take years to accomplish.

Once he dealt with Cipher's lackey, Logan Fortunato, and whatever fools they sent out into the desert to kill him, then he too would disappear and become anonymous again. He, Joe Pullo, and Jake Caliber won their first encounter with Cipher. He intended to win this one as well. After that, Cipher could live with the defeat and forget about him or they could be stupid and actively try to harm him.

He hadn't been out to cause them trouble but had run afoul of them while minding his own business. If they wanted to make that personal, then so be it.

Cipher had resources but so did he. If Cipher had left a trail somewhere that could be followed back to them, Tim Jackson would find it. Tanner was sick and tired of having to defend himself against large criminal organizations. He didn't give a damn what they did as long as they left him and his alone. By operating in Stark, even in such a limited and transitory manner, they had involved him. If they were as smart as he'd been told, they would see that they had nothing to gain by angering him and back off. He intended to send that message by destroying the next kill squad they sent at him. There would be swift death delivered with no shred of mercy.

∼

Tanner had parked an old travel trailer near an abandoned salt mine. There was a single road with a cracked surface that led in and out of the area. Creosote bushes dotted the landscape and other than the trailer there was only one other structure that was about three hundred yards away. The miners had left behind a concrete building whose roof had collapsed a long time ago.

Tanner and Henry were in that building. They

had been waiting for hours for something to happen. Prior to that, they had spent time preparing for an attack.

Fortunato would have assumed that Boss and his people were dead and might have even seen mention of it in the news. He would know that meant that Tanner had Weber and that they might still be together. Thanks to the deception that Weber birthed, Fortunato would think that he knew Weber's new location. He would be sending people to kill Tanner and abduct Weber.

"How many do you think this Fortunato will send after you?" Henry asked.

"Likely a dozen or more, but it won't matter if they send a hundred."

"Are you angry?"

Tanner looked at him, then sighed. "I'm tired of this. I became Tanner so that I could take contracts and make money by doing the world a favor and ridding it of a few scumbags. I never wanted to become the target of every group of fools who saw me as a way to build their reps."

Henry shrugged. "It's unavoidable."

"What is?"

"Becoming a target. You're the seventh Tanner. You've got the experience of Spenser and the other Tanners to call on, and Cody, you're just an undeniable badass. It would be amazing if you *weren't* a target for every jerk looking to build a name or prove something."

"You're saying that this had to happen?"

"Yeah. Each Tanner was better than the one before them. Over time, someone like you was bound to come along and be so much better than everyone else. You've told me about the Scallatos, about Maurice Scallato, and how he, his father, and several generations before them were all trained as assassins. Maurice Scallato was their Tanner Seven. He was not only gifted at being an assassin, but he had been trained to be so. Maybe he felt the same way you did. Maybe that's why he went around killing other assassins who he felt were a threat to taking his title as greatest assassin of all time. It could be that he felt it was kill or be killed."

"Do you really believe that?"

Henry smiled. "No. I've read Jacques Durand's book. Scallato was just an asshole. And he bit off more than he could chew when he went after you."

Tanner smiled back at him, as his anger faded. The smiled dimmed as he realized something.

"This could be your life someday too, do you understand that? As a Tanner, you'll always be a target for somebody."

Henry shrugged. "Let them come. If I'm even half as good as you then they won't stand a chance."

"I'm serious, Henry. You might have to prove

yourself over and over just like I do. Think about that and know that I won't blame you if you decide to quit being trained by me."

Henry looked at his mentor with a solemn expression. "Cody, all I've ever wanted is to be just like you. You're the best man I know, and I'll pay any price to make you proud of me. I know I told Crash that I'm a long way from being named Tanner Eight, and I sure as hell am, but... I want it bad, man. I want to be a Tanner so much that I can taste it."

"I know that feeling."

They went back to watching the horizon for signs of movement. It was eighty-three degrees and heat was rising off the desert floor. Off to the west, a group of turkey vultures were circling. If they were in search of carrion, they would soon have a plentiful supply.

Henry's young ears detected the sound an instant before Tanner registered it. Motorcycles.

~

HOMBRE WAS EAGER TO GO UP AGAINST TANNER. HE knew that if the Diablo's Doubles killed the hit man that he would have guys fighting each other to join the motorcycle club. He liked being the leader and all, but things hadn't been the same since the old leader of the club, Bronco, had been killed by Jake

Caliber. If he could double, or better yet, triple the club's members, he might take a trip to New York City with them all and hunt down that bastard Caliber.

Hombre had led a hard life. Not once had it occurred to him that most of his troubles were his own fault. The problem was a common one. Hombre was stupid. That stupidity was about to land him in the worst trouble of his life.

~

"HOMBRE," TANNER SAID. HE HAD RECOGNIZED THE club leader after viewing him through the binoculars.

"You know one of those guys?"

"Their leader is someone I've seen before. His luck has just run out."

"They're headed straight for the trailer," Henry said, then he watched through his own pair of binoculars for what he knew was about to happen.

Tanner hadn't wanted the fishing line and fishhooks to go fishing. They were to be used as the first of the traps that Tanner and Henry had laid for any would-be attackers.

~

Hombre and the other members of the motorcycle club slowed as they neared the travel trailer, then began circling it from fifty feet out. Not one of the men wore a helmet, as it wasn't mandatory in Texas.

Hombre had arrived with twenty-one other men. He felt confident that Tanner and the man named Weber had probably ducked inside the trailer when they heard them coming. Someone was in there for sure. There was a car parked nearby, and a folding chair and table were set up outside by the steps. There were two bottles of beer on the table, indicating that there was more than one person inside.

Hombre stopped his bike and cut off the engine, then he made a slicing gesture at his throat that told his followers to cut their engines too. When it was quiet, Hombre sent a blast from a shotgun into the front of the trailer. Buckshot shattered a window and blew holes in the curtain that had been behind it.

"Hey in there, come on out or we'll come on in there and drag your asses out."

There was no answer, but the faint sound of a radio could be heard playing from inside.

"All right, we'll do things the hard way." Hombre started up his motorcycle and his men did the same as they took out their weapons.

Clothes hung on a line, as if to dry in the sun. It was not the only line that had been hung.

As Hombre rode closer to the trailer, he opened his mouth to shout an order to the man beside him. As he did so, he felt something sharp cut his tongue and felt a tug at his upper lip. Still more pain erupted along his face and throat, even as he saw the other man's right cheek rip open. Cries of pain were all around him. At the same time, three of the men lost control of their bikes and caused accidents. One of the men who had fallen off his ride had some sort of hook jammed in an eye. His scream was loud enough to overcome the sound of the engines.

"Fishing hooks! The damn things are everywhere," one of the other bikers said as he pulled one from the crook of his elbow and a another from his scalp.

Tanner and Henry had run super thin fishing line from the trailer to several of the nearby cane cholla trees and also tied the ends to some of the hardier scrub brush. The hooks themselves were difficult to see until you were right up on them. Since Hombre and his men had been riding their bikes instead of walking, they ran into the hooks' sharp ends at greater speed. The trap had been meant to annoy, confuse, and cause minor injuries. Tanner had originally intended to add a series of traps that would maim and whittle down any force arrayed against him. When the odds were more manageable, then he would have opened up with a sniper rifle and picked off those that remained. However, the more he thought about Cipher's attempts to kill him, the madder he became. Henry had been right. Tanner was angry, and he was all out of patience.

~

Hombre fought his way through the hooks and made it to the door of the trailer. His shotgun made short work of the lock and he swung open the door. There was no one inside that he could see. What he did see were a stack of what looked like bricks of clay. They were on the floor. Sitting atop the stack was some sort of electronic device with a glowing red light. Hombre figured out that the clay wasn't really clay at the same time the red light turned green. One tenth of a second after that and Hombre was all but vaporized by the detonation of plastic explosives.

~

"Holy shit!" Henry said. He had watched the trailer explode and devastate anything within a hundred feet of it. Additional explosions occurred when the trailer's propane tanks blew up, along with the motorcycles' gas tanks. Sections of the trailer were flung into the air along with body parts. The Diablo's Doubles Motorcycle Club had just ceased to exist.

When the dust that had been stirred up had settled, Henry looked through the binoculars. What he saw was a scene from a nightmare.

"That should send a message to Cipher," Henry said in a voice that was almost a whisper.

"We're not done yet."

"Oh, right."

There was a second bomb in the old car. It had been flipped over onto its roof by the shock wave of the first blast and had no window glass left. The second bomb was inside its trunk. Tanner hit a button on the detonator he had and activated the second bomb before the turkey vultures had swooped in for a meal. He had nothing against the birds, who were just doing what they had been designed to do.

Tanner hadn't known what sort of force or in what numbers they would have been thrown at him. Hombre and his twenty-one leather-clad imbeciles could have turned out to be even more men than that. The pair of detonations had been set-up to devastate a hundred or more.

Tanner dropped the detonator and used his boot to grind it into the sand. "Let's go."

They left the ruins of the old concrete building and walked over a hill. Their vehicle, a pickup truck rented under an alias, had been camouflaged to blend in with the landscape and go undetected during a search of the area. Hombre had never bothered to look for it. He led his men toward the trailer without any consideration that things weren't what they looked like. Once they had the truck uncovered, Henry settled in the passenger seat.

"I know there were a lot more men this time and that we were prepared for them, but that seemed too easy."

"It was."

"Why?"

"Fortunato may have underestimated me again or he might have been trying to make me think a certain way."

"You mean like make you overconfident?"

"Yeah… maybe."

Tanner started the truck. There were backpacks, sleeping bags, and other camping gear in the rear. If they were stopped, they could claim they had been hiking in the desert. Once they were back in range of the cell phone towers, Tanner's phone alerted him that he had a text. It was from Tim Jackson, and it supplied Tanner with the home address of the man calling himself Logan Fortunato, Guy Hutchinson.

"I'll be taking a different flight while you fly

home, Henry. Tim Jackson has found Guy Hutchinson."

"Let me come with you."

"You've got early classes tomorrow and I don't know how long this might take."

"Where is Hutchinson?"

"He's in Aurora, Illinois."

"Is that near Chicago?"

"Very close. I'll take a flight there and drive to Aurora."

"The guy who nearly ran me over, Gage Kline, is from Chicago. Do you think there's a connection?"

"I'll find out if there is."

∽

HENRY'S FLIGHT TO BROWNSVILLE LEFT AHEAD OF Tanner's plane to Chicago. Before leaving, Henry asked a question. "Once you've dealt with Fortunato, will all this be over?"

"I'm not sure. Boss and his men, Diablo's Doubles, they were just part of a bigger plan that's already in motion. I think the next shoe will drop whether Fortunato is dead or not."

"He sent over twenty guys last time. What's next, an army?"

Tanner smiled. "That would be the natural assumption, wouldn't it?"

"But you don't think so?"

"I won't assume so. I'll be on guard for anything."

"You've been fed a steady diet of fast balls, and now you think he might throw you a curve, is that it?"

"Something like that."

Tanner's flight was called. He boarded it while considering the possibilities of what he might find in Illinois. Fortunato could have a team of security personnel guarding him, or he might be deadly in his own right. The truth turned out to be something that Tanner had never expected.

18

OPEN HOUSE

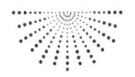

Guy Hutchinson lived midblock on a street of quiet homes that all cost somewhere in the neighborhood of a million dollars. His house was made of brick and had a stone walkway with an adjacent cobblestone patio.

The home was lit up brilliantly and the blinds had been left up to allow a view inside. There was also a note taped to the door. It was four words written in black magic marker on a sheet of white paper.

WELCOME, TANNER. I'M UNARMED.

Tanner was viewing the note through a pair of binoculars. He was parked on the block behind the house that was across the street from Hutchinson's home. A view through a wrought iron fence allowed him to see down a driveway and across to Hutchinson's front door.

Tanner pondered the note. If it was a trap, it was an odd one. Twice he had seen a man walk past one of the windows. The man was tall, good-looking, had a mustache, and seemed to be pacing while smoking a cigarette. He matched the description of Hutchinson that the hapless pilot of the helicopter had given him.

Tanner watched the home for a few more minutes before driving off to park closer. An hour later he had done a thorough reconnaissance of the area and had uncovered no traps or signs of bodyguards or snipers. It was possible that the homes on either side of Hutchinson could be filled with armed men waiting to pounce, but that seemed unlikely.

A bickering couple and two young kids had left the home on the right an hour earlier. From their strident conversation Tanner had learned that they were going to visit the wife's mother. In the home on the left side, a preteen girl and her friends entered the house while staring at their cell phones. When the girl opened her door to enter, her younger brother had wet the girls down with a water gun. Of course, if you wanted to make things appear harmless, staging those two events would do the trick.

Tired of playing the waiting game and watching, Tanner strolled up Hutchinson's stone walkway and raised his hand to ring the doorbell. He hesitated at the last instant and knocked instead in case the doorbell button was rigged to deliver a lethal electric charge.

Tanner grunted. Hutchinson's welcome sign was turning him into a paranoid. He would have felt much better about things if there had been a trio of thuggish-looking armed guards standing on the front steps.

The home had a pair of decorative, leaded glass doors at the entrance. Tanner could make out a shape approaching. It was a man, and although he couldn't make out fine details through the opaque glass, he could see enough to know that man had nothing in his hands. The figure stopped ten feet from the door and asked a question. The voice was deep and resonant.

"Who's there?"

"I'm the man you left the note for."

Silence, then, "The door's unlocked. Please don't shoot me."

Tanner wondered if the doorknob was electrified but then reached out and turned the damn thing anyway. He was tired of playing games.

Hutchinson swallowed audibly as their eyes met,

then he smiled when he saw that Tanner's hands were empty.

"The note worked. That's good. And if you let me explain I know you'll see that you have no reason to kill me."

"Why would you believe that? You've sent at least two teams of men to slaughter me. Why shouldn't I kill you?"

Hutchinson held up his hands at chest height. "That wasn't me and I can prove it."

∼

Minutes later, Tanner was in Hutchinson's living room listening to a recording of the conversation that Hutchinson had had with the real Logan Fortunato. Before entering the room, Tanner told Hutchinson to lower all the window blinds. They then walked together as Tanner checked the home to make certain they were alone. When he was satisfied that there was no one lying in wait, ready to ambush him, they returned to the living room. They listened in silence as the recording played. Hutchinson's baritone voice was contrasted against the man he was speaking with, whose voice was levels higher and carried with it a tone of condescension.

"I don't want anything to do with Tanner. If you're going after him, I won't be helping you."

"You truly are afraid of this man?"

"I am. I also don't plan to commit suicide by challenging him."

"Cipher is an important client. We make millions by servicing them and they're offering three times the usual fee for dealing with Tanner. If I refuse this contract, the relationship we've built with them will be in jeopardy."

"Yeah, but you'll go on breathing. If you fail to kill Tanner, he'll kill you."

"Hutchinson, if you abandon me like this there will be consequences."

"I don't want to end our association but there are risks I won't take. If the police arrest me someday, I'll do time, yes, but I'll still be alive. That's not true if Tanner gets me in his sights."

"Fine. Quit. But remember this, I'll make you pay a steep price for it."

Hutchinson laughed. "Logan, you won't be alive to follow through on the threat. Not if you insist on going up against Tanner."

"You're a coward!"

"A live coward. Goodbye, Logan. Remember that I warned you when Tanner catches up to you."

Tanner listened to the recorded conversation. He had one question when it ended.

"How do I find the real Fortunato?"

"That I don't know, but I do know how you might be able to track him down."

"If this is some sort of trick or a plan to walk me into a trap, you're making a mistake."

Hutchinson shook his head furiously. "No traps and no tricks. Tanner, you just heard the conversation I had with Logan. I knew that the only way to survive you was to plead for mercy. I never sent anyone to kill you and I told Logan that he would regret doing so." Hutchinson pointed at the tape player. "Logan Fortunato thinks that there's no one his equal. I've known for a while that his ego and hubris would get him killed someday. He thinks he's untouchable because he's never been seen and no one but me even knows that he exists. He's got everyone believing that I'm him, so that when trouble came, I would be the one in the crosshairs."

"You signed up for that, didn't you?"

"I did, and I've been paid extremely well to put myself in peril. Going up against you was a risk I was unwilling to take."

"How do I track down Fortunato?"

"We were talking on the phone one day when I heard a voice in the background. It was a voice that I knew. She's a high-priced call girl named Gianna. A night with Gianna will cost you dear but she's worth every penny."

"What do you expect me to do, abduct this woman and make her tell me where Fortunato lives?"

"That would work, but it may not be necessary. Gianna will book a single date, but she also has a few regulars. If Logan is one of those regulars, Gianna could be followed right to him."

"A woman like that would have a handler, a pimp of some sort. She would also have someone watching her back."

"Jerome," Hutchinson said.

"Who's Jerome?"

"He's the guy who drives Gianna to her appointments. He introduced himself to me the first time I paid for Gianna's services. He made a point of letting his jacket slip open so that I could see the gun he had strapped to his belt."

"Describe Jerome."

"He's a black man, a little taller than you and maybe carrying more muscle. He's no hoodlum. He spoke well, dressed nicely, and he knew that print on the wall over there was a Matisse."

Tanner looked at the picture. He had studied art briefly as he tried to be knowledgeable about many things. If he'd been asked, he would have said that it was an early work of Pablo Picasso and not Henri Matisse.

"So, you're saying Jerome is intelligent. That's good. A smart man will know when it's in his best interest to share information."

"You're going to question Jerome?"

"Yeah, and you're going to help me get to him by making a date with the hooker."

"But if I do that Jerome might guess that I set him up."

"He might. Listen, Hutchinson, you've been doing Logan Fortunato's dirty work for years and now you expect to walk away clean? I won't kill you if you help me get to Fortunato, but I don't give a damn if somebody else does it. If you think this Jerome will want revenge then take a trip or move away. You're lucky I haven't beaten this information out of you just for the hell of it."

Hutchinson nodded. "Maybe it is time that I found new pastures." He smiled. "At least I'll have one more night with Gianna."

∼

Hutchinson sent a text off to the call girl. He told Tanner that she usually responded within an hour. It took her thirty-seven minutes to accept his request, but she wouldn't be able to see him until four days later. Tanner was both pleased and annoyed by the delay. He wanted to end things as quickly as possible but would enjoy being able to spend time at home. He'd been away quite a bit lately.

"I'll be back in four days," Tanner said as he was leaving. "If you run, I'll find you."

"I'm not going to run."

"Do you know what make and model car Jerome drives?"

"I never really caught a good look at it, but I think it's a black Lexus. He parks in my driveway while he's waiting."

Tanner tossed a thumb at the sign on the door. "How many days has that been there?"

"Two days. The mailman asked me who Tanner was."

"What did you tell him?"

"I said that you were an assassin. He laughed and waved his hand at me."

"People seldom believe the truth when they hear it."

Hutchinson nodded. "I've noticed that too."

19
QUEEN'S GAMBIT

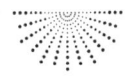

After he'd been back on the ranch for one day, Cody was tempted to say the hell with Fortunato and not return to Illinois.

That would be a mistake. Fortunato and others might view his disinterest for reluctance to face another attack. If anyone ever thought that he feared a challenge, those seeking to build a rep would crawl out of the woodwork to take a crack at him the next time he stuck his head up. Fortunato had to be put down. His death might make Cipher reconsider their stance to treat him as an enemy. After all, whoever Logan Fortunato was, he was hiding behind a shield of anonymity just as the leaders of Cipher were. If he could be found and killed, why not them?

Cody had been out for an early run when his phone alerted him that he had received a call on another phone that he owned. The other phone was a burner that he'd been using lately. Henry had the number and so did Crash, but neither of them would be calling so early. They would also call his real number, which they both had. There was one other person he had given the burner phone number to, Karl Weber.

Tanner stopped running and listened to the voicemail message. It wasn't from Weber. It was from his daughter, Amelie. She sounded as if she'd been crying and was out of breath.

"Mr. Tanner... this is Amelie. I need your help again. Oh, I hope you get this message. My father and I thought we were... we thought we were safe, but these men attacked us... and there were so many of them. Papa tackled one of them so that I could get away and I've been running all night. If you get this message, please come get me. I'm at the Regal Diner in Dallas. Oh God, I'm so scared."

The message ended. Tanner wondered why Weber had stayed in the Dallas area. Then he remembered the regret Weber displayed over having to give up the farmland he had inherited. He might have stayed in the area while trying to find a way to profit from that asset. If so, greed had been his downfall.

Cody couldn't call Amelie from his own phone, so he returned home to call her on the burner phone that was in his desk.

∼

The call was answered on the first ring. "Tanner?"

"Yes. Are you safe?"

"I think so. Can you help me?"

"Tell me what happened."

"Papa was lying about getting on a bus and leaving. For some reason he wanted to stay in the city for another day so that he could talk to a lawyer. I think it had something to do with the farm."

"When were you attacked?"

"We were staying at a motel when we heard noise and loud voices coming from the parking lot. We looked outside to see a lot of men wearing suits going door to door. They looked like police detectives or federal agents, but their cars didn't have those flashing lights. Papa recognized one of them and knew that he worked for the people who were after us."

"Is that when you ran?"

"Papa and I slipped out of the room, but we were

seen by one of those guys. Papa told me to run and I took off across the road while he fought with the man. I... I heard shooting. I pray that Papa is all right."

"How many men were there?"

"Dozens. They were everywhere. The motel is a huge place with over a hundred rooms and two floors, but it seemed like they were near every room that we could see."

"Are you still at the diner?"

"Yes. How soon can you get here?"

"I'm not nearby, but I can get to you in about four hours."

"Four hours? Oh God, that's going to seem like an eternity."

"You could go to the cops and they would keep you safe."

"They'd also arrest me."

"Yeah, they would, but you would be alive."

"I don't want to go to the police."

"Stay put and I'll get there as soon as I can. If you have to leave, then call me and tell me where you've run to."

"Hurry, Tanner, please?"

"I'm coming."

In Dallas, Amelie smiled as the call ended. Tanner was on his way and he didn't suspect a thing. Weber's statement that Amelie had gone through a rebellious streak in her teens had been an understatement. Amelie had run away often, was involved with drugs, and had been with one man who was a career criminal.

She had been only sixteen at the time, but she hadn't been an innocent who was led astray. She'd been a party girl, a high school dropout, and it was Amelie who had planned the crime she and her lover had committed.

Weber had made certain she never wanted for anything but was never there when she needed him. It was because of that neglect from her father that Amelie gravitated toward older men. One of those men was an ex-con named Willie Ralston. Ralston was thirty-one when he met sixteen-year-old Amelie. Ralston had served time for armed robbery after he and a friend robbed a check cashing business. Amelie talked him into committing another crime. The kidnapping of a former classmate.

The victim's name was Tonya Flores. Tonya was the only daughter of Juan Flores. Juan had come to Dallas from Puerto Rico at eighteen and gotten a job as a janitor and dishwasher in a restaurant. By the time he was forty-five he owned seventeen restaurants and two hotels. That was also the year he married and became a father. Juan adored Tonya and spoiled her. Tonya never wanted for anything. She was beautiful, a talented pianist, and became head cheerleader. Amelie hated her with a passion. She and Tonya had never exchanged two words, but Amelie despised her all the same. She couldn't stand it that one of her peers had it so much better than she did. It wasn't fair.

On a night when Tonya was driving home alone after visiting a friend, Amelie drove up behind her at a red light and purposely bumped into her with the stolen car she was driving. Tonya stepped out of her yellow sportscar to see what damage had been done.

Amelie had wondered if Tonya would recognize her, but the other girl displayed no reaction indicating that she remembered her. That angered Amelie. It shouldn't have. She and Tonya had only one class together the year before Amelie had dropped out of school, a school that had over two thousand students. Amelie had also cut that class almost as many times as she had shown up for it.

Willie Ralston pulled up in a van and asked if he could help. When Tonya turned to look at him, Amelie slammed a wrench against the back of her head, knocking her out.

A witness who viewed the scene at a distance said that he thought Tonya had fainted. The tall and leggy

Tonya had obscured his view of the smaller and petite Amelie.

That same witness heard Willie Ralston holler at Amelie, although he couldn't make out what he said. Ralston was angry because he'd been afraid that Amelie had killed their hostage before the girl could make a video begging her father to pay the ransom.

Ralston lifted Tonya off the street and lowered her into the van. Then he hollered at Amelie again, to tell her to get in back of the van and make sure that Tonya didn't wake up and start screaming.

Tonya had survived the attack and made the plea to her father that he pay the ransom. As is often the case, the kidnapping fell apart when Ralston went to pick up the ransom. He shot an FBI agent in the foot before being gunned down.

Amelie had seen it all happen from up on a hill where she had been waiting for Ralston. She had followed him to make sure he didn't try to run off with the ransom and keep it all for himself. Now there was no money, no Willie, and the cops would be going to the garage apartment he rented as soon as they ran his prints and figured out who he was.

Amelie went back to the apartment where she paced for six minutes as she thought over her options. Because she was a minor, Ralston had always snuck her in and out of his place in the back of the van. As far as Amelie knew, no one was aware of their relationship. She'd been living with Ralston while her father assumed that she had run away again. She hadn't run away; she had just never returned home one day, the way a pet cat might do.

A plan formed in Amelie's mind and she put it in motion without hesitation. Tonya was lying on a mattress in a corner of the bedroom. She was trussed up, blindfolded, gagged, and drugged into unconsciousness. Amelie found a hammer in a toolbox under the kitchen sink and used it to bash in the back of Tonya's head. While doing so she had put on one of Ralston's jackets and pulled the hood closed tightly around her face. The blood spatter that struck her washed off easily. The remainder of the blood stained Ralston's jacket and implicated him in the crime. The act of murder meant nothing to Amelie. She had never hesitated in swinging the hammer once she had made her mind up to kill. If anything, there was pleasure in killing Tonya, whom she'd envied.

Afterward, she stripped naked then removed the handcuffs off of Tonya's corpse and secured an end around her left wrist. The apartment was one big room with a partitioned area for a tiny kitchen and another for the bathroom. Amelie walked every inch of it to make sure that there was nothing she had overlooked. When she was in the bathroom, she saw the bottle of sleeping pills that Ralston had bought to drug Tonya with.

Amelie downed three of the pills. It was a huge dose considering how little she weighed, but she felt it was worth the risk. Besides, the cops had to be headed her way at any minute. Returning to the bedroom, Amelie laid on the bed and secured the free end of the handcuffs to the brass headboard. When the cops arrived, they would find one dead kidnap victim and a teen runaway who had been handcuffed to a bed, drugged, and raped. Amelie knew her father was nowhere as wealthy as Tonya's father, but he wasn't a poor man either. It wasn't inconceivable that Ralston might have abducted her as part of a second kidnapping scheme. The rape was as big a lie as the rest of it, but Amelie had sex with Ralston right before he left to get the ransom and she had not showered since.

Amelie felt a chill as she lied on the bed naked and waiting for the cops to show. The drugs had yet to kick in and make her groggy, but she became aware of another sensation. She had to urinate. She decided that being found lying in her own urine would only make her story more believable and giggled as warm fluid was released.

She was having trouble keeping her eyes open when the apartment door burst inward, and FBI agents flooded into the room. They read the scene just as she hoped they would and treated her as another of Ralston's victims.

The witness who'd seen the abduction had told the investigators that he thought Ralston had another girl and that he'd been ordering her around. His statement gave credence to Amelie's tale of being treated like a slave by Ralston.

There was a brief period where she thought it might all unravel when Ralston's junkie brother, Frank, came forward and claimed that Amelie and his brother had been lovers and that the kidnapping was her idea. Being thorough, investigators looked into the allegation. And yes, while Amelie and Tonya had attended the same high school and shared a class together briefly, there was no other evidence that they had ever interacted in a friendly or unfriendly manner. It was also difficult for the FBI agents involved in the case to view the delicate and lovely teen, Amelie, as someone capable of committing such actions. Frank was threatened with a charge of giving false testimony and backed off. He would overdose on heroin fourteen months later and be found dead in an alley.

Logan Fortunato had been following the story in the news. Unlike the FBI, he believed Frank Ralston. He'd seen something familiar in Amelie when she gave an interview about her ordeal to a local reporter. The girl lied as well as he had when he was her age and confronted by his elders.

Fortunato hired a female private investigator to follow the girl. It wasn't long before he received a report that stated Amelie was sleeping with a married man, doing drugs, and shoplifting.

Those activities were a far cry from kidnapping and murder, but it was enough for Fortunato. He decided to recruit Amelie and used a surrogate to approach her and make her an offer.

Amelie was to play a small role in the burglary of an expensive home by distracting the man hired to guard it. She did her part well, accepted money, and asked if they had other work for her. Over time, Fortunato had asked more and more of Amelie, including murder. She would do anything as long as she felt the compensation was enough. By the time she was nineteen, Amelie had become Fortunato's favorite assassin. The girl killed without mercy and because of her small size, youth, and beauty, her victims suspected nothing until she struck. Anyone seeing her driving around in the car with the vanity plates and teddy bears would never suspect what she was. She was a sociopath who could fake emotions she didn't feel and cry on cue.

Gage Kline certainly hadn't seen her coming. After going separate ways with Bohdan Kushnir and Cory Sparks, Kline had contacted a friend he knew who might be able to tell him why the rare bill they'd stolen was too hot to fence.

That "friend" was connected with Fortunato and knew that he was looking for the heist crew. When his contact described the woman he had spotted Kline with, Fortunato was certain that she was the blonde seen in the video taken by a drone. Cipher had sent him a copy of that video along with other pertinent information and reports about the robbery. If Gage Kline refused to give up his partners, maybe the woman would talk.

Fortunato had also accepted a contract on Tanner. With the robbery crew grabbed and the rare bill recovered, Fortunato could then turn all of his attention toward killing Tanner.

Kline and the woman were tortured and told all they knew about their partners. It wasn't enough to be able to track them down. Fortunato then had a brilliant idea. Amelie Weber and the blonde woman involved with the heist crew were similar in appearance. He'd had that very thought while watching the drone video. He was also aware of Weber's peripheral involvement in the heist. Amelie's father acted as a courier for rare items that Cipher used to launder funds. Fortunato had been aware of that when Amelie had first come to his attention. He'd been gathering information for years on Cipher's operatives. He had a long-range plan to take over their operation someday. That would only happen if he could identify who they were, which so far had been impossible to do.

But he did know about Karl Weber's connection to Cipher, as did Amelie. One of her standing assignments was to spy on her father for Fortunato. That was why he knew that Weber had been the courier on the day of the heist.

His fertile mind saw a way to use Weber, Amelie, and the surviving members of the heist crew to lure Tanner into the perfect trap. It meant sacrificing the reliable Boss and his team, but in the interest of killing Tanner, they were an acceptable loss.

∼

AMELIE WAS TOLD WHAT HER PART WAS TO BE, AND SHE was excited by it. She'd heard of Tanner and it pissed her off that he was considered to be the greatest assassin of all time. She was an assassin too and had killed nearly eighty people since bashing in Tonya Flores's skull. To her, Tanner was another Tonya. Someone who other people held in higher esteem than herself. It would be a pleasure to kill the bastard, and she could get back at her father at the same time.

Things had gotten scary there for a while when Boss attacked. Amelie didn't think the hit crew was aware that she and they were working for the same man. Still, by attacking, they gave her a chance to see Tanner in action. And who knew he had a boy wonder? Tanner had been impressive, as had the boy called Henry, but Amelie considered herself better than both of them.

Fortunato was right. Played correctly, Tanner would never see her coming. He would show up at the diner to play the big hero and when they were alone, she would slit his throat wide open. She wouldn't use a knife. To place him at ease she was wearing a pair of tight shorts and a form hugging top. If she had a concealed weapon on her it would be easy to spot. She'd have a weapon, nonetheless. It would be the silver barrette that she'd taken off the blonde who had been involved in the heist. She'd sharpened one side of it until it was honed to a fine edge. At some point, Tanner would look away or turn his back on her. When that happened, Amelie would use the barrette to kill him.

She had already used it once, on her father. Amelie smiled again. The look on her old man's face had been priceless.

With her father dead, the farmland he'd inherited would pass on to her, along with most of his money. And once she killed Tanner, then those in the know would have to respect her. And better yet, they would fear her. Things were certainly looking up. And soon Tanner would be facedown.

Amelie sent off a text to the number she'd been given. She wanted to let Fortunato know that Tanner was on his way and would soon be dead.

A text came back moments later. It consisted of only two words.

Don't fail!

Amelie smirked. Of course she wouldn't fail. Tanner thought of her as a not too bright and harmless piece of fluff. When she sank her makeshift knife into his throat, those intense eyes of his would be wide with wonder.

Amelie sat at a small table inside the diner and ordered a piece of cherry pie. When it came, she imagined the redness of the cherries was Tanner's blood.

20

DEVIL IN DISGUISE

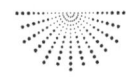

LUCK WAS WITH TANNER AND HE WAS ABLE TO GET A flight to Dallas that had him arriving at the diner a little more than three hours after speaking to Amelie. He'd driven by once to take in the surroundings and saw nothing and no one that looked suspicious or as if they were keeping watch.

The car he was in was nondescript and had been ordered in advance from a black-market service that supplied vehicles, weapons, and other items their customers might need. They didn't operate in every state, and only in certain cities. Tanner wished they would expand. Despite the steep prices they charged, the service was A+ and there were a number of times he could have used them over the years. If he returned the car and the weapons he'd ordered in good condition, he would receive a discount the next time he used the business.

He paid a yearly fee for a similar arrangement based in Europe. It was one he rarely took advantage of, but when he needed it, he really needed it. Such was the nature of insurance, legal or illegal.

Amelie had certainly been watching for him. She ran from the diner before he could step out of the rental he was driving. A look of relief was evident in her eyes and she heaved a sigh as she took the seat beside him.

"Thank you for coming. I didn't know who else to call or what to do."

Tanner looked her over and saw that her eyes were red, and one hand was fiddling with the silver barrette in her hair. He had the car in motion and drove around to park at the side of the diner, and away from the windows where people sat in booths to look out at the highway.

"I want to go to the motel where you were staying, Amelie. It's possible your father could still be there, or someone there knows what happened to him."

"Oh, Papa. Do you think he's still alive?"

"I don't know. But I will find out and I'll get you somewhere safe. Do you still have that new ID your father bought?"

"No. It was left in the room."

"Let's hope the cops haven't found it."

"Yes," Amelie said.

∼

AMELIE WAS WAITING FOR THE PERFECT MOMENT TO act. By pulling around to the side of the building, Tanner had cut down on the number of possible witnesses. She would still be bloody after she killed him. That couldn't be helped and was something she hadn't considered before. It didn't matter. Killing Tanner was the important thing, once that was done, she'd worry about getting clean of his blood.

Tanner placed the car in drive and drove forward slowly. There was a narrow one-way street at the rear of the diner. The car's GPS had designated it as a first step along the shortest path to reach the motel they were headed to. As he turned away from her to see if anyone was coming down the street, Amelie made her move and freed the sharpened barrette from her hair.

It should have worked. She should have been able to take him unawares and inflict a fatal wound before he knew what was happening. Three factors saved Tanner as they had many times in the past.

Factor one: The man was inhumanly fast. His hand speed didn't only help him be quick with a gun but in all forms of self-defense.

Factor two: He was a Tanner, the seventh Tanner and had been trained to be on guard at all moments and against all persons. Tanner could walk in a room and his mind would automatically count the number of people present and look about for any threats. He had no reason to mistrust Amelie but that didn't mean he had classified her as harmless. She was a human. Human beings were always capable of violence.

Factor three, and the one most applicable: Tanner, decades earlier, had been betrayed before by a woman. She had been someone he trusted with his life and loved deeply, and she had been willing to kill him when she deemed it necessary. Since that day, trust had come very hard for him.

As he was turning his head to glance away from Amelie, Tanner had used the button on the door to adjust his side mirror so that he could also have a view of what was in the other direction. This was something that Spenser, his one-eyed mentor, did often while driving. Tanner adopted the habit whenever he was driving with someone other than those few he trusted implicitly. Amelie was not numbered in that class.

The first thing he saw was her twisted features as she freed the barrette. The innocent face had hardened, and her pouty lips were curled into a sneer. The barrette was in the shape of a heart. The bottom of the heart had been sharpened to a fine edge.

Tanner hit the brakes and at the same time gripped Amelie's delicate wrist; the one that was connected to the hand holding the edged weapon. Panic flared in Amelie's green eyes as she struggled uselessly. Tanner slammed her hand against the dashboard and the barrette fell onto the floor. The fingers on her free hand were curled into claws and she was reaching out to scratch at his eyes while emitting a sound of anger. Tanner released her wrist, batted away her hand, then hit her hard on her chin. Amelie collapsed like a toy whose batteries had fallen out.

∼

A LOOK AROUND TOLD TANNER THAT NO ONE HAD seen the brief struggle inside the car. He drove off and headed to a nature preserve that was less than half an hour away. He hit Amelie hard enough to keep her out that long, and likely much longer.

Fortunato had sent seven men after him, a biker gang, and finally, a young woman who might weigh a little over a hundred pounds. Judging by her previous interactions with him, Tanner had to assume that she'd been Fortunato's ace in the hole all along. As strategies went, it was a damn fine one. He'd had no reason to suspect Amelie or fear her. He guessed that belief had been shared by whoever she had killed before attempting to murder him.

Maybe someday a woman should be named a Tanner. They certainly had an edge in the advantage of doing the unexpected when it came to being an assassin.

Hutchinson said that Fortunato believed he had no equals. That conviction might have merit if this level of guile was an example of how he normally operated. The plan had been brilliant, and if his reflexes had been slower, Amelie's improvised blade might have found its way into his throat. Fortunato was not someone to take lightly.

~

BY THE TIME AMELIE STIRRED THE SUN WAS SETTING. She was still in the car. Tanner hadn't bothered tying her up, but her sneakers had been removed and she was sitting on a blanket that had been spread out over the seat. Tanner was parked on a gravel surface. He'd been headed to the nature preserve when he spotted a vacant warehouse with a huge gravel parking lot. The building was in the midst of a renovation and the work crews had left for the day. If Amelie bolted from the car and tried to run in her stocking feet on the uneven stones, she wouldn't get far.

Her eyes came into focus slowly as she moved her tongue around in her mouth. When she turned her head, she saw that Tanner was holding a gun in his right hand. The weapon had a silencer attached. In his left hand was a baton. It was retracted in on itself, but the heavy metal ball at its top was in plain view.

Amelie moaned. "Shit, my jaw hurts, and I can taste blood."

"Is your father a part of this?"

Amelie looked at the gun, then smiled at Tanner. "You don't want to kill me, and I don't want to die. Why don't we make a deal?"

"What sort of deal?"

"The kind of deal a man and a woman can make," Amelie said. As she spoke, she had unfastened the top button on her blouse. Tanner snapped the baton open with one flick of his wrist, and with a second flick he smashed the baton against Amelie's fingers. She yelped, then cradled her left hand with her right.

"Ow! That fucking hurt."

"Here's the deal. I ask questions and you answer them. If you don't answer, you get hit. Where's your father?"

"He's dead, all right."

"You killed him?"

Tanner had lowered the windows despite the dropping temperature. He did so to provoke a reaction from Amelie. It worked, and she wrapped the blanket around her shoulders.

"Why are the windows down? It's getting chilly outside."

"Tell me about your father."

"I had to kill him, okay? He was in the way. Now that he's dead, I'll inherit all that land my aunt left him. There's money too, Tanner. I could pay you to let me live."

"Who are you working for?"

Amelie looked as if she were going to stall or make up a lie. After a small shrug, she answered. "The guy calls himself Logan Fortunato."

"Have you ever met him?"

"No. He's just a voice on the phone, or usually a text."

"And do you work for Cipher too?"

"You know about Cipher?"

Tanner raised the baton an inch. Amelie got the message and answered the question.

"I don't work for them, but my father did and so does Fortunato."

The silver barrette was sitting in a cupholder. Tanner tapped it with the baton.

"How did you get this?"

"Gage Kline was stupid and went back to

Chicago where people knew him. Someone ratted him out and I was sent there to deal with him. The chick that owned the barrette was there with him. I think her name was Sandra. Fortunato noticed that she and I look alike, so I pretended to be the woman who was seen in that video."

"The video taken by the drone?"

"Yeah."

Tanner filed that information away. It meant that Cipher was capable of getting copies of police evidence, likely through hacking into the department's computer files.

"And you killed Kline and Sandra?" he asked Amelie.

She smiled. "I dressed like a maid but with a really short skirt and Kline let me into his hotel room while the woman was off somewhere. Dude swore he was going to get some from the slutty maid, but instead, I slid a knife between his legs and cut it off. When the woman returned, I did her too, after torturing her. That stuff I wrote down for you was all she and Kline knew, which was nothing."

"It was enough to find the other members of the crew and get the rare bill back."

"Shit. Really? Fortunato will be pissed about that. How the hell did you track them down? All I told you was that one of them had a dog and that the guy with the beard liked soup."

"Like I said, it was enough. How involved was your father in all this?"

"My father had nothing to do with that robbery, but he knew that Cipher might blame him, and he panicked and went on the run."

"Then you tracked your father down and pretended that you were involved and needed help?"

"Yeah."

"If he didn't tip off the second heist crew, then who did?"

"It was that slut, Sandra. She was sleeping with Marco Deering, but she'd also been screwing a guy from the other crew, David Gonzalez. She'd overheard him talking to one of his partners about the heist and told Marco about it. I guess she liked him better than Gonzalez. It was just bad luck that they both showed up at that festival at the same time."

"What you said before, you were wrong."

"About what?"

"About me not wanting to kill you." Tanner pulled the trigger twice while shooting at an upward angle. Both rounds entered Amelie's cold heart and it ceased beating. The slugs had passed through her small body, the blanket draped over her shoulders, and went out the window. Eight minutes later she was wrapped up inside the blanket and lying hidden beneath scraps of wood and pieces of discarded wallboard inside a construction dumpster. Her passing had left behind a few drops of blood that were easily wiped away.

Tanner kept her phone. Her other phone. It received a text that had to have been sent by Logan Fortunato.

Is Tanner dead yet?

Tanner debated sending a reply and decided not to do so. He would be talking to Logan Fortunato when he returned to Illinois. In the meantime, let the man wonder what happened to his femme fatale. After dropping the car off where it could be retrieved, he took a cab to the airport and was back home on the ranch in time to have dinner with his family.

21
LET'S MAKE A DEAL

AT MIDNIGHT, LOGAN FORTUNATO WAS IN HIS PRIVATE chambers brooding while sipping on Scotch. He had taken Amelie's failure to reply as proof that she was dead. Fortunato wished that he could bring her back to life and kill her again for ruining his brilliant plan. The damn girl must have overplayed her hand or acted impulsively. Whatever her error had been, it had brought about disaster.

Tanner still lived and to make matters worse, the rare bill was in the hands of the police. The final members of the heist crew were also in police custody. Failure, there was failure everywhere and it simply could not be tolerated.

Maybe he couldn't get the currency back or negate the fact that the police found Cory Sparks or

Bohdan Kushnir before he could, but he could still find a way to kill Tanner.

He set his drink down on the edge of the desk. He needed a clear head if he were to come up with another plan to kill the hit man. And he would take his time. Tanner presented no personal threat because there was no way that he could find him. Fortunato closed his eyes and let the tension drain away. He would conceive of another plan; one that didn't rely on a woman to make it work.

Thinking of women brought to mind an image of his sex toy, Gianna. They would have their date in a few days, and he was looking forward to it more than usual. Sex always relieved his tension and stress and being with the whore soothed him in a way he didn't quite understand.

Fortunato thought about Amelie again. Like Boss and his team, the little wench would be difficult to replace, and it was all because of Tanner.

Fortunato smiled. He'd incorporate torture into his next plan to deal with Tanner. The man deserved to suffer for causing him grief. Fortunato opened his laptop to play a game of chess online. There was an expatriate in Japan who was always up for an impromptu game.

Before long Fortunato was immersed in a challenging match and had pushed the issue of Tanner to the back of his mind.

GIANNA TURNED OUT TO BE A DARK-HAIRED BEAUTY. Tanner saw nothing to indicate that she would be worth more than any other good-looking whore. He'd been with hundred-dollar hookers and a couple of call girls who were in Gianna's league. The Giannas of the world didn't earn ten to fifty times more because they were that much better looking or responsive in bed. They earned their money for what they did outside the bedroom. They made the man they were with feel like the most important person in the world and used flattery and sympathy in equal measure.

Most people considered themselves to be a good person deep down. They also felt as if fate were picking on them at times. This was true of a saintly priest or of someone serving six consecutive life sentences for murdering children.

If Gianna was as good as Hutchinson claimed, she would have picked up on the difference in his mood since the last time she'd seen him. She would sense that he was tense, worried, and she might even intuit that his life circumstances had changed. Knowing that would give her ample opportunity to express concern and lift his spirits with adulation. By the time they wound up in bed, Hutchinson would be much more positive about his future, and he would again think that Gianna was the greatest sex partner a man could ever have.

Tanner had been immune to the flattery of the call girls he'd been with. They had also found him impossible to read emotionally. He had never paid for the women, not at those prices. They had been a gift for fulfilling contracts.

He'd always been closed lipped about his feelings and was never one to talk without reason. He wasn't about to start unburdening himself to a woman whom he'd met only minutes earlier and whom he might never see again. But, for many men, that was the call girls very appeal. It was like they weren't real people. You didn't fear running into them at a restaurant or in the supermarket. Call girls were a fantasy come to life. They would not only allow you to do what you wanted to them in bed, but they made you feel like they just might give a damn about you. They didn't, no more than the men they were with cared about them, but it was the game they played, the life they led, and it sure paid better than being a waitress.

~

IT HAD TAKEN TANNER TWO MINUTES OF STARING AT Jerome until he recalled where he had seen him before. It had been 2008 and Jerome had been Jerry, a bone breaker for a loan shark in New York City. Hutchinson had stated that Jerome wasn't a hoodlum. He'd been half-right. He wasn't your *average* hoodlum.

Tanner eased up alongside the car and tapped on the side window. Jerome startled, then stared. When he realized who he was looking at, he lowered the window.

"I hope you're not here to kill me, Tanner."

"You're in luck; it happens to be my night off."

Jerome smiled. "What the hell are you doing in Aurora?"

"I'm here on business. How did you wind up here?"

"After that shit that went down in New York City I decided it would be a good time to make a change. I knew some people in Chicago and went there."

"The last time I saw you the doctors said that you'd never walk again, Jerry."

"The doctors say a lot of things, but they were damn near right. It took eight months before I was well enough to take a step and another year before I could run a little. And hey, Tanner, call me Jerome."

"I have a favor to ask, Jerome."

"Take a seat and we'll talk." Jerome clicked open the locks on the door. Hutchinson's guess had been wrong. The car was a black Mercedes, not a Lexus.

Tanner got inside and told Jerome that he was looking for one of Gianna's clients.

"You're going to kill this guy?"

"That's right. He's tried to kill me at least twice. I figure I owe him no less in return."

Jerome rubbed a hand over his chin. "I'll bet you it's the guy that Gianna calls the chess master."

"Is he a professional chess player?"

"I don't know, but she says that he talks about it all the time. She took up the game and read several books on the subject so she would be able to understand him better. You know, at this level, the girls are more like therapists than whores."

"Yeah. But why is he the client that came to mind when I said that I'm looking for a man who hires killers?"

"About nine months ago Gianna came down with the flu and had to cancel about a week's worth of dates. I went around visiting her list of regulars to explain why she would have to cancel. The chess master was one of them. I had only talked to him once before. That was the first time he and Gianna had a date. I always make sure that they know she has someone watching her back. The dude was smiling at me, Tanner, and I could tell he wasn't afraid. That's unusual. Most of these guys look nervous or nod like they understand. Not that bastard, he practically shut the door in my face, and he's a little dude. I was bigger than he is when I was twelve and playing Pop Warner football. Anyway, I tell him about Gianna being sick and he tells me that she should take better care of herself if she wanted to keep him as a client. I just nodded and turned to walk away but he calls me back. He had something he wanted to say."

"Was it an apology for being rude?"

Jerome laughed. "Not exactly. The asshole told me that if he wanted to, he could have me killed, and that I was never to bother him again. I resisted the urge to beat the little fucker to death and left. Gianna doesn't like him either. She charges him twice the going rate and he pays it every week."

"Does she visit him on the same day?"

"She'll be there tomorrow at eight."

"No, she won't. There won't be any point in visiting a dead man."

"What if he's not the right guy?"

"I'll figure that out before I kill him, but I think your instincts are right."

"He tells Gianna to call him Lawrence, but he's never given her a last name and always pays in cash."

"Where can I find him?"

"I'll give you directions. It's about an hour from here, near Rockford."

Tanner got the directions, asked a few more

questions that concerned details he needed to know, then opened his door to leave the car.

"Take care of yourself, Jerome."

"I'm living the easy life. Guarding Gianna is much better than dealing with deadbeats."

"A woman in her line of work has a short career after she ages a little."

"Yeah, but this business never lacks new recruits. When Gianna retires, I'm sure they'll give me a new girl to look out for."

"Job security is a good thing."

"Hey, do you ever see Joe Pullo anymore?"

"We keep in touch."

"Tell him I said hi."

"I'll do that."

"And Tanner?"

"Yeah?"

"Make that little bastard hurt some before you kill him. It pissed me off when he threatened me."

"I know how you feel."

~

The following evening, a black Mercedes backed into the driveway of Larry Evers, the man who called himself Logan Fortunato.

Jerome told Tanner that he always backed down the two-hundred-foot driveway, and any other driveway so that if needed, he could pull out quickly. The Mercedes Tanner drove was the same model and year of Jerome's vehicle. Tanner had also doctored a pair of stolen license plates so that they matched the alpha-numeric characters found on Jerome's Mercedes.

A cardboard container holding four cups of hot coffee were perched on the dashboard. The steam from the coffee fogged up the windshield and side windows in case Fortunato had hidden cameras. After parking, Tanner waited.

If Gianna's customer, Lawrence, was also Logan Fortunato, he would grow impatient and wonder why his rented date was keeping him waiting. The front door of the home opened at four minutes after eight and a short man with a small frame stood in the doorway looking out at the car. Tanner could see him in the rearview mirror but remained unseen because of the fogged glass and tinted rear windows.

When nothing else happened, the man stomped toward the vehicle. As soon as he reached it, he tapped on the side window with his knuckles. Tanner couldn't see his face because of the steam but there was no mistaking the anger displayed by his body language.

He lowered the window. A flash of confusion showed on Fortunato's face, but it was replaced by shocked recognition. Fortunato had seen the old mugshot of Tanner and the sketch of him that had been passed around years earlier.

His mouth moved wordlessly for a moment before he mumbled out, "Tanner... I..."

"Hello, Fortunato," Tanner said. As he spoke, he fired a Taser.

~

"WE CAN COME TO AN ARRANGEMENT," FORTUNATO said.

Tanner was screwing a silencer onto the end of his gun. "I like the arrangement we have now."

Fortunato was lying on his back in the driveway. Tanner stood over him with a gun aimed at his head.

"I'm talking about money. Surely a million dollars is worth more to you than revenge."

"I could have both if I tortured you to give me the million dollars."

"Cipher!"

"What about them?"

"I could help you locate them. They're the ones you want. I was simply hired by them to do a job. I personally have no animosity towards you."

"You say you can help me locate them. How would you do that?"

Fortunato plucked a phone from his shirt pocket. "They communicate with me on this phone via text. The next time they make contact I'll set up a trap."

"What sort of trap?"

"I... I don't know, but I'll think of something."

"Your last trap—trying to kill me—didn't work out very well for you. Why should the next one do any better?"

Fortunato couldn't think of a reply, but he was desperate to stay alive and determined to come up with something that would keep Tanner from killing him.

"I could work for you."

"Doing what?"

"Anything. You name it. Anything."

"Would you like to know how I found you?"

"Um, all right."

"First, Guy Hutchinson convinced me that he wasn't you. After that, Jerome told me about you. He said that you threatened him."

"Jerome?"

"Gianna's bodyguard and driver."

"The large black man. I didn't like him. He tried to intimidate me."

"He asked me to make sure you suffered before I killed you."

The gun fired once, and Fortunato screamed as the slug buried itself in his left knee.

Minutes passed before Fortunato was able to

speak. Tears of pain had wet his cheeks and his voice was hoarse from his screams and crying. He raised up a hand.

"Tanner... don't hurt me again."

"That shot to the knee wasn't for Jerome. That was for me. Goodbye, Fortunato."

Tanner's next two bullets were fired at Fortunato's head.

~

HE SPENT HOURS INSIDE THE HOUSE. HE HAD NO problem getting past Fortunato's security measures. In his haste to leave the house and confront Gianna for keeping him waiting, Fortunato had left the door to his office sitting wide open.

Tanner took Fortunato's laptop. He would send it along with the cell phone Fortunato used to Tim Jackson. Maybe the hacker would find something on them that could help lead Tanner to Cipher's doorstep, but he doubted it. Whoever was in charge of Cipher hadn't stayed anonymous by being careless.

For now, their threat was ended, the rare bill was recovered, and he had performed the favor that had been asked of him. It was time to go home.

22

AND THE WINNER IS...

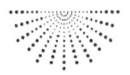

Steve Mendez lost the race for Mayor of Stark by less than thirty votes. At the same time, he was reelected as Chief of Police by ninety-one percent of the voters. It was apparent that the good citizens of Stark would rather have him protecting them than leading them.

Mendez felt disappointed and flattered at the same time. He also felt bad for his deputy chief, Clay Milton. By remaining in office, Milton would be unable to advance.

"You'll beat Jimmy next time, Chief," Clay told him. "And in the meantime, I know that there's still a lot more I can learn from you."

Jimmy Kyle's acceptance speech was anything but modest. He acted as if he had won by a wide margin and was a beloved leader. When he showed up at the police station to gloat, as usual, he had Councilwoman Avery beside him like a shadow. Avery had also eked out a victory over her opponent.

Jimmy made a point of telling Mendez that he would be cutting his budget again. When Mendez told him about the rare bill that would be auctioned off and the proceeds becoming the police department's discretionary funds under the forfeiture laws, Jimmy's good mood was dimmed. Mendez pointed out something else.

"Fergus Jones won a seat on the town council when he beat one of your toadies. You may find that the council won't go along with your budget suggestions as easily as they have in the past."

Fergus Jones disliked Jimmy because Jimmy had once broken the heart of Fergus's baby sister. He had replaced a member of the town council who had rubberstamped Jimmy's proposals.

Jimmy realized the truth of Mendez's words. His good mood had fled completely. "We're out of here," he told Councilwoman Avery.

Mendez watched them go. With his friend Fergus on the town council to give Jimmy hell, the next four years might not be so bad. And remaining Stark's Chief of Police wasn't the worst thing in the world.

~

TIM JACKSON'S SEARCH OF FORTUNATO'S COMPUTER uncovered Fortunato's real name of Larry Evers and several overseas bank accounts, along with a hefty stock portfolio. Tanner told Tim to drain it all and send him half the money. Tim told him that he was the best boss ever.

BABY MARIAN TOOK HER FIRST STEPS ON Thanksgiving Day. She released the arm of the sofa she'd been holding onto and toddled over to her mother. Sara had tears in her eyes when she picked her up. It seemed to her that the children were growing up too fast.

EARLY IN DECEMBER, CODY WAS AT HOME WHEN HE got a call from Henry.

"The news is reporting that a message was placed in the want ads of every major newspaper in the country yesterday. Cody, I think it might have been aimed at you."

Cody had been at his desk with the computer on. He did a search and found the story. People were baffled by the short message and wondered who it was meant for. It read:

T, you mind your business, and we will mind ours, C.

Cody was unconvinced that it concerned him until he read further into the story. All of the ads were placed by someone named Cy Fore, and traced to a fictitious company in Asia named Tan Nor.

Cipher was asking for a truce. They'd probably spent the last several weeks trying to track him down without success and were worried he might have been busy doing the same. It wouldn't have escaped their notice that he had located and killed Logan Fortunato, a man who had also considered himself anonymous and untraceable.

A ceasefire was fine by him. Neither he nor Cipher had deliberately gone after the other but instead had found themselves at cross purposes twice. If they stayed out of his way, he'd be happy to return the favor.

Despite that, Tanner had no intention of attempting to respond to the message. Let them worry and wonder if he was lurking out there somewhere, on the hunt for them, or poised to strike.

He smiled. A little fear might do the bastards some good.

TANNER RETURNS!

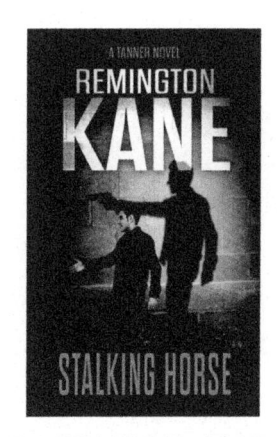

STALKING HORSE - BOOK 40

AFTERWORD

Thank you,

REMINGTON KANE

JOIN MY INNER CIRCLE

You'll receive FREE books, such as,

SLAY BELLS – A TANNER NOVEL – BOOK 0

TAKEN! ALPHABET SERIES – 26 ORIGINAL TAKEN! TALES

BLUE STEELE - KARMA

Also – Exclusive short stories featuring TANNER, along with other books.

TO BECOME AN INNER CIRCLE MEMBER, GO TO:
   http://remingtonkane.com/mailing-list/

ALSO BY REMINGTON KANE

The TANNER Series in order

INEVITABLE I - A Tanner Novel - Book 1

KILL IN PLAIN SIGHT - A Tanner Novel - Book 2

MAKING A KILLING ON WALL STREET - A Tanner Novel - Book 3

THE FIRST ONE TO DIE LOSES - A Tanner Novel - Book 4

THE LIFE & DEATH OF CODY PARKER - A Tanner Novel - Book 5

WAR - A Tanner Novel- A Tanner Novel - Book 6

SUICIDE OR DEATH - A Tanner Novel - Book 7

TWO FOR THE KILL - A Tanner Novel - Book 8

BALLET OF DEATH - A Tanner Novel - Book 9

MORE DANGEROUS THAN MAN - A Tanner Novel - Book 10

TANNER TIMES TWO - A Tanner Novel - Book 11

OCCUPATION: DEATH - A Tanner Novel - Book 12

HELL FOR HIRE - A Tanner Novel - Book 13

A HOME TO DIE FOR - A Tanner Novel - Book 14

FIRE WITH FIRE - A Tanner Novel - Book 15

TO KILL A KILLER - A Tanner Novel - Book 16

WHITE HELL – A Tanner Novel - Book 17

MANHATTAN HIT MAN – A Tanner Novel - Book 18

ONE HUNDRED YEARS OF TANNER – A Tanner Novel - Book 19

REVELATIONS - A Tanner Novel - Book 20

THE SPY GAME - A Tanner Novel - Book 21

A VICTIM OF CIRCUMSTANCE - A Tanner Novel - Book 22

A MAN OF RESPECT - A Tanner Novel - Book 23

THE MAN, THE MYTH - A Tanner Novel - Book 24

ALL-OUT WAR - A Tanner Novel - Book 25

THE REAL DEAL - A Tanner Novel - Book 26

WAR ZONE - A Tanner Novel - Book 27

ULTIMATE ASSASSIN - A Tanner Novel - Book 28

KNIGHT TIME - A Tanner Novel - Book 29

PROTECTOR - A Tanner Novel - Book 30

BULLETS BEFORE BREAKFAST - A Tanner Novel - Book 31

VENGEANCE - A Tanner Novel - Book 32

TARGET: TANNER - A Tanner Novel - Book 33

BLACK SHEEP - A Tanner Novel - Book 34

FLESH AND BLOOD - A Tanner Novel - Book 35

NEVER SEE IT COMING - A Tanner Novel - Book 36

MISSING - A Tanner Novel - Book 37

CONTENDER - A Tanner Novel - Book 38

TO SERVE AND PROTECT - A Tanner Novel - Book 39

STALKING HORSE - A Tanner Novel - Book 40

THE EVIL OF TWO LESSERS - A Tanner Novel - Book 41

SINS OF THE FATHER AND MOTHER - A Tanner Novel - Book 42

SOULLESS - A Tanner Novel - Book 43

The Young Guns Series in order

YOUNG GUNS

YOUNG GUNS 2 - SMOKE & MIRRORS

YOUNG GUNS 3 - BEYOND LIMITS

YOUNG GUNS 4 - RYKER'S RAIDERS

YOUNG GUNS 5 - ULTIMATE TRAINING

YOUNG GUNS 6 - CONTRACT TO KILL

YOUNG GUNS 7 - FIRST LOVE

YOUNG GUNS 8 - THE END OF THE BEGINNING

A Tanner Series in order

TANNER: YEAR ONE

TANNER: YEAR TWO

TANNER: YEAR THREE

TANNER: YEAR FOUR

TANNER: YEAR FIVE

The TAKEN! Series in order

TAKEN! - LOVE CONQUERS ALL - Book 1

TAKEN! - SECRETS & LIES - Book 2

TAKEN! - STALKER - Book 3

TAKEN! - BREAKOUT! - Book 4

TAKEN! - THE THIRTY-NINE - Book 5

TAKEN! - KIDNAPPING THE DEVIL - Book 6

TAKEN! - HIT SQUAD - Book 7

TAKEN! - MASQUERADE - Book 8

TAKEN! - SERIOUS BUSINESS - Book 9

TAKEN! - THE COUPLE THAT SLAYS TOGETHER - Book 10

TAKEN! - PUT ASUNDER - Book 11

TAKEN! - LIKE BOND, ONLY BETTER - Book 12

TAKEN! - MEDIEVAL - Book 13

TAKEN! - RISEN! - Book 14

TAKEN! - VACATION - Book 15

TAKEN! - MICHAEL - Book 16

TAKEN! - BEDEVILED - Book 17

TAKEN! - INTENTIONAL ACTS OF VIOLENCE - Book 18

TAKEN! - THE KING OF KILLERS – Book 19

TAKEN! - NO MORE MR. NICE GUY - Book 20 & the Series Finale

The MR. WHITE Series

PAST IMPERFECT - MR. WHITE - Book 1

HUNTED - MR. WHITE - Book 2

The BLUE STEELE Series in order

BLUE STEELE - BOUNTY HUNTER- Book 1

BLUE STEELE - BROKEN- Book 2

BLUE STEELE - VENGEANCE- Book 3

BLUE STEELE - THAT WHICH DOESN'T KILL ME- Book 4

BLUE STEELE - ON THE HUNT- Book 5

BLUE STEELE - PAST SINS - Book 6

BLUE STEELE - DADDY'S GIRL - Book 7 & the Series Finale

The CALIBER DETECTIVE AGENCY Series in order

CALIBER DETECTIVE AGENCY - GENERATIONS- Book 1

CALIBER DETECTIVE AGENCY - TEMPTATION- Book 2

CALIBER DETECTIVE AGENCY - A RANSOM PAID IN BLOOD- Book 3

CALIBER DETECTIVE AGENCY - MISSING- Book 4

CALIBER DETECTIVE AGENCY - DECEPTION- Book 5

CALIBER DETECTIVE AGENCY - CRUCIBLE- Book 6

CALIBER DETECTIVE AGENCY – LEGENDARY – Book 7

CALIBER DETECTIVE AGENCY – WE ARE GATHERED HERE TODAY - Book 8

CALIBER DETECTIVE AGENCY - MEANS, MOTIVE, and OPPORTUNITY - Book 9 & the Series Finale

THE TAKEN!/TANNER Series in order

THE CONTRACT: KILL JESSICA WHITE - Taken!/Tanner - Book 1

UNFINISHED BUSINESS – Taken!/Tanner – Book 2

THE ABDUCTION OF THOMAS LAWSON - Taken!/Tanner – Book 3

PREDATOR - Taken!/Tanner - Book 4

DETECTIVE PIERCE Series in order

MONSTERS - A Detective Pierce Novel - Book 1

DEMONS - A Detective Pierce Novel - Book 2

ANGELS - A Detective Pierce Novel - Book 3

THE OCEAN BEACH ISLAND Series in order

THE MANY AND THE ONE - Book 1

SINS & SECOND CHANES - Book 2

DRY ADULTERY, WET AMBITION -Book 3

OF TONGUE AND PEN - Book 4

ALL GOOD THINGS... - Book 5

LITTLE WHITE SINS - Book 6

THE LIGHT OF DARKNESS - Book 7

STERN ISLAND - Book 8 & the Series Finale

THE REVENGE Series in order

JOHNNY REVENGE - The Revenge Series - Book 1

THE APPOINTMENT KILLER - The Revenge Series - Book 2

AN I FOR AN I - The Revenge Series - Book 3

ALSO

THE EFFECT: Reality is changing!

THE FIX-IT MAN: A Tale of True Love and Revenge

DOUBLE OR NOTHING

PARKER & KNIGHT

REDEMPTION: Someone's taken her

DESOLATION LAKE

TIME TRAVEL TALES & OTHER SHORT STORIES

TO SERVE AND PROTECT
Copyright © REMINGTON KANE, 2020
YEAR ZERO PUBLISHING, LLC

This book is a work of fiction. Names, characters, places and incidents either are products of the author's imagination or are used fictitiously.

Any resemblance to actual events or locales or persons, living or dead, is entirely coincidental.

All rights reserved. Except as permitted under the U.S. Copyright Act of 1976, no part of this publication may be reproduced, distributed or transmitted in any form or by any means, or stored in a database or retrieval system, without the prior written permission of the publisher.

❀ Created with Vellum

Made in the USA
Middletown, DE
12 February 2025